Hood Tales Volume 1:

Maid for You and Robin the Hood

Hood Tales Volume 1:

Maid for You and Robin the Hood

C. N. Phillips

www.urbanbooks.net

Urban Books, LLC
300 Farmingdale Road, NY-Route 109
Farmingdale, NY 11735

Hood Tales Volume 1: Maid for You and Robin the Hood
Copyright © 2017 C. N. Phillips

ISBN 13: 978-1-62286-619-9
ISBN 10: 1-62286-619-3

First Trade Paperback Printing December 2017
Printed in the United States of America

10 9 8 7 6 5 4 3 2 1

This is a work of fiction. Any references or similarities to actual events, real people, living or dead, or to real locales are intended to give the novel a sense of reality. Any similarity in other names, characters, places, and incidents is entirely coincidental.

Distributed by Kensington Publishing Corp.
Submit orders to:
Customer Service
400 Hahn Road
Westminster, MD 21157-4627
Phone: 1-800-733-3000
Fax: 1-800-659-2436

Hood Tales Volume 1:

Maid for You and Robin the Hood

by

C. N. Phillips

Maid for You

Chapter 1

That .40 get to dancin', I carry it on my hip
I ain't gon' feel no pressure, don't care how these
niggas feel

Ava Dunning drove like a madwoman through the parking lot of her job trying to find a parking space. The black '99 Impala she whipped rattled and jumped violently as she hurriedly ran over a pothole in the pavement. She was already fifteen minutes late, and the crammed parking during the dinner hours wasn't helping her at all. She finally found a spot when an elderly couple left the restaurant, and Ava turned into it before anyone else could.

Used to kiss my granny, make my morning
swerves
Foggy window in my Cutlass was my learning
curve
Keep a couple pistols in my furniture

She nodded her head and rapped along with Nipsey Hussle before she cut the car off.

Ava hopped out and half walked, half jogged to the front door of the establishment, a place called Buckets. It was a popular restaurant in the city of Omaha, Nebraska. It had been open for six months, and Ava could probably count on one hand how many times she'd been on time to work. She scoped the crowded restaurant until she found her manager across the dining room having a hearty discussion with a few patrons. Ava ducked her head down and hurried to the employees-only part of the building.

"Damn, girl! You always late!"

Ava rolled her eyes as soon as she heard Damien's feminine voice targeted in her direction. She hadn't even been in the room for five seconds, and he was already on her neck and getting on her nerves. Ava was glad her boss, Amanda, was nowhere in earshot because he would have definitely outted her.

Damien was tall and skinny for his height. If it weren't for the goatee and mustache he rocked, he would have been the spitting image of a Ninja Turtle. He must have recently gotten his hair cut, because it wasn't disheveled like it usually was, and his line-up was crisp. Damien was an openly gay man, and honestly, the only friend Ava had in the place.

She put her coat alongside the other employees' in the closet they all shared and grabbed a blue apron to cover her white collared blouse. She pulled her long ponytail through the back of the baseball cap they were all required to wear at work. It was blue and white and had the words BUCKETS TEAM MEMBER on the front of it.

"Shut up," she said when she turned back to face him. "You're always worried about somebody else but yourself."

"I can be worried when you were supposed to be here almost twenty minutes ago, and I've been covering your tables."

"My bad, Damien," she groaned even though she wanted to snap at him again. If the tables had been turned she would be irritated too, so she couldn't even be mad. She grabbed a notepad with a pen attached to it from one of the walls in the employee break room. "I was at OPPD trying to pay the light bill. I didn't think it would take that long."

"Well, what matters now is that you're here and it's Friday night!" he said, shrugging his shoulders. "It's like a damn zoo out there."

"I saw. Amanda is out there talking to a table in my section."

"About them . . ." Damien gave Ava a look that had "warning" written all over it. "I just brought them their food out, and the wife says, 'I didn't know there was bacon on my mashed potatoes.' Bitch! What the hell do you think comes on loaded mashed potatoes? Then the husband complained about his steak and, honey, that steak looked so damn good when I brought it out I almost took a bite my damn self. Oh, my God, girl, I'm just glad you're here. Those people are irritatin'! That tip isn't even worth it!"

"Is it just us tonight?"

"Yes, and Joey. But that fat mothafucka is probably in the back sneaking sautéed shrimp again!"

Ava found herself grinning as they both revealed themselves from the back room. They walked down the hallway together, and the loud croons of the radio blended in with the conversations of the customers. Once on the dining floor, the two parted ways to man their own sides of the restaurant, and Ava did her best to steer clear of her manager.

It was a hectic night, as to be expected on a Friday night, but Ava did well on her tips. One thing about Ava was that she was a people person. She could have a conversation with a wall and make it feel like it was standing up in the right place. Even the table Damien had warned her about took well to her and tipped her well when they left. With $200 in her pocket, she was feeling pretty good and had successfully ducked Amanda for half of her shift. Her luck ran out when she was caught off guard as she was clearing a table off. The sound of someone clearing their throat behind her made her stop wiping the table off in mid-stroke.

"You were late today. Again."

Ava turned around and found herself face to face with the coldest blue eyes she'd ever seen in her life. Amanda stood before her, firm, and gave her employee an intense stare down. What she had said was a statement and not a question, and Ava stood there knowing that she was busted.

Amanda was a white woman of average height, with cherry blond hair and a tan that made her skin almost orange. She wore a two-piece tan pantsuit and short, pointed-toe heels. She wasn't the most beautiful woman, but after about ten drinks one might think she was as beautiful as Britney Spears. Her hands were clasped in front of her as she waited for what was sure to be a BS response.

"I'm sorry, Amanda." Ava put her hands up. Droplets of water flew since she had completely forgotten that she was holding a wet towel. Quickly, she set it down and swallowed the lump in her throat. "I tried to be on time today, I really did. Traffic was a monster today."

"That's what you said last time, and I thought we agreed that you'd leave your house ten minutes earlier from now on."

"And I did, but I got caught up paying a bill for my mom. I'm sorry. It won't happen again."

"If this doesn't sound like a broken record, I don't know what it sounds like." Amanda shook her head with a clenched jaw. "Look, Ava, you're a very bright girl, but I can't keep allowing you to come in when you feel like it. This is a business, and it's not fair to the other employees. One more chance and, if you mess it up this time, you're gone. Understood?"

"Yes, ma'am."

"Good. Now finish here and go see what table fifteen needs."

***

There was loud thumping coming from the house when Ava pulled into the cracked driveway. All the lights were on, and there were at least five cars parked on the street outside of the home she lived in with her mother. She rolled her eyes since she'd already experienced a long night at work and the last thing she wanted to come home to was a house full of people. She groaned when she opened the front door and the skunky smell of marijuana mixed with fried chicken danced at the tip of her nostrils. At the front door, there were two ways to go: upstairs, or downstairs to the basement. She opted to go up, toward the commotion.

Right off the stairwell, the kitchen was straight ahead, the living room was to the right, and the hallway that led to the three bedrooms was to the left. The living room and kitchen were filled with drunk people having the time of their lives. Ava found her mother sitting at the head of the oval kitchen table smoking a joint and holding a hand of cards.

"Boo Boo!" she cried when she saw her daughter standing at the top of the stairs still in her work clothes. "Come on in here and show these mothafuckas how we get down in Spades!"

"Nah, Mama." Ava shook her head, trying to hide her irritation. "I'll pass. You have a good time, though."

She eyed all of the women and men in the house and recognized them as all of her mom's friends throughout the years. No matter where they lived, their house was always the "kick it" spot, and for as long as Ava could remember, she hated it. She always felt that her mother, Alaya "Lay Lay" Dunning, was too good to hang around the people she did. And she definitely felt that her mom was too pretty to be with her boyfriend, Rick Dumphy, who was sitting right next to her, drunk out of his mind.

Alaya was a woman in her late forties, but she looked no older than a dirty thirty. She had pretty golden-brown skin and kept her straight hair cut short. Everyone told her she resembled Halle Berry in her earlier career. She was a little on the thick side, which must have been where Ava inherited her own thick thighs from; and she had a smile that could keep a man by her side forever.

"Aw, let her go to her room," Dumphy shouted, and he threw his hand in Ava's direction. "Don't let her ruin the party! When is she movin' out, babe?"

His comment rubbed Ava the wrong way, and what irritated her more was that her mother answered his question with a shrug. She didn't check him for coming at her only child disrespectfully at all; instead, she leaned forward, kissed him, and said the word, "Relax." Maybe it was the alcohol in her system, or maybe the weed had a grasp too tight on her mind; either way, Ava felt her anger surge.

"I'll move when you can afford to help out around here," she spat at the fifty-year-old man. "I could have moved out a long time ago but, unfortunately, she's forty-somethin' years old and can't keep the damn lights on! *And* she has a grown-ass man living up in here with a whole job."

Instantly, everyone in the house got quiet, and the volume of the music was turned down. Ava didn't realize she had been yelling until the very last word was out, but she didn't care. What she said was the truth. The only reason she still lived at home was because her mother needed her to. She wasn't responsible; and, instead of paying all her bills, Alaya would pay some and spend the rest of her check turning up with her friends all month.

The sound of chair legs scraping the floor filled the air as Dumphy scooted back in his seat and stood up.

His eyes were fiery as he looked at her like she was the scum underneath his shoes. Standing at six foot two, he towered over everyone in the kitchen and wrinkled his dark forehead. Alaya had always been attracted to men with chocolate complexions, but Dumphy by far was the darkest she'd ever brought home. The hair on his face, which was in need of a trimming, mixed with the dingy wife beater and blue jeans, made him look rough.

Turning his nose up at Ava, he shook his head. "What, you think you better than me or somethin'?"

"Nah." Ava shrugged her shoulders. "I just think I'm more responsible."

"More responsible, huh?" He laughed to himself and glanced down at Alaya. "If she was more responsible she wouldn't be a community college dropout, right, baby? Bitch must be dumber than a box of bricks, ain't that what you said?"

The entire house erupted into laughter, and Ava turned to her mother with hurt in her eyes. She couldn't believe Alaya would tell Dumphy her business; more so, she couldn't believe her mom would say such hurtful things about her. Alaya was laughing too until she saw the hurt expression on her daughter's face.

"Boo Boo, I—"

"Stop!" Ava put her hands up. "Just stop! I'm tired of this shit! How the fuck do you let your man talk to your daughter like that? Nah! How do you let him disrespect the person who is literally keeping the lights on in here? If I hadn't paid the three hundred dollars to OPPD today all you mothafuckas would be in the dark right now."

"Boo Boo—"

"Noooo, Mom! No! Don't 'Boo Boo' me right now. I was going to wait until the morning to ask, but now seems like the right time." Ava clenched her purse in her hands a little tighter, trying to contain her frustration. "I have been giving you money to cover the electrical bill for three months now. How did we get behind?"

"Um, well, baby, Rick needed the money to handle some business. I was going to pay the bill with my next check."

Ava lost it.

"You've been givin' this bummy-ass nigga my money? This old, dirty mothafucka! He ain't my boyfriend, he's yours! And you got me sponsoring his musty ass."

"Wait a damn minute!" Alaya threw the cards in her hands and jumped to her feet. She pushed a few people out of her way until she was standing toe to toe with her daughter. "You better watch your mouth in my damn house! If I wanna give him money, I for damn sure will!"

"You mean this house? The one I had to cosign for?" Ava spat back. "You always letting these men dick-whip you! Got you out here broke!"

"You ungrateful little bitch!"

Alaya's hand came out of nowhere and struck Ava so hard in the face that her neck snapped to the right. She raised her hand to strike her again, but Ava caught her hand in midair.

"I have nine reasons under my pillow right now why you aren't going to touch me ever again," Ava snarled and threw her hand back. "I never in my life thought I'd see the day my own mother would turn on me, but you know what? Fuck you and this raggedy-ass nigga. I'm out."

Ava turned her back on her mother and went to her room to pack her things. She had no idea where she was going to go, but she knew she had $1,500 in the bank and another $500 on hand. In an hour, she packed up most of her belongings, including the pistol she bought off the streets, and took them out to her car.

"If you leave, don't come back!"

Ava had just slammed her trunk shut when she looked up to see her mother and Dumphy leering at her from the doorway. He had his arms wrapped tightly around Alaya's waist and had a smirk on his face like he'd won something. Ava flicked both of them off and told them to go to hell.

"When he starts whoopin' your ass like all the other ones did, don't call me!" Ava yelled back, opening her car door. "Fuck you!"

She didn't wait to hear what nastiness would come out of Alaya's mouth next. She just plopped down in her seat and headed to the Ramada Inn off of Seventy-second Street. They didn't have the best rooms, but they were affordable and comfortable. Right then, all she could ask for was comfort.

Chapter 2

"Now what?" a middle-aged, pecan-colored man asked the person standing beside him. The night was still young, but they'd gotten done with their task a lot sooner than expected. Both men stood in the middle of what looked to be a war zone but was really a living room covered in blood and dead bodies.

The smell hadn't settled in yet, and King Dex was happy that the design of the home wasn't all white like the last time. He and his right-hand man, Dorian, had come to pay an old friend a visit at a home in West Omaha to settle a score. The man, Edward Franklin, owed King Dex a big chunk of paper and had been ducking him for months. If he thought that lying low and not making too much noise would get him out of a debt with the devil himself, he was dangerously mistaken. There wasn't enough security in the world that could keep King Dex away from his money. The still-smoking gun hanging in his hand at his side proved that.

He and Dorian had come in as a two-man team facing an army of at least ten. There was a time, long ago, when those odds would have intimidated Dorian. He wouldn't have believed they would win. However, when King Dex took him under his wing, he told him, "No lion should be afraid to go into a lion's den. For when he enters, he is at home." Their eyes circled the room for anyone with a still-moving chest and didn't stop until they were certain everyone was deceased.

"Call the cleaning service. Tell them to get here pronto," King Dex answered in a low, baritone voice. "They will only have an hour tonight to remove all evidence."

Dorian nodded his head as he pulled his cell phone from the pocket of his blue Giorgio Armani suit. He scoffed and shook his head when he saw a few drops of blood on his shoes. They were brand new, and he really liked them. He made a mental note to order a new pair as soon as he got home. He walked outside, leaving King Dex standing alone in the living room.

"Old friend," King Dex said, shaking his head at where Edward lay face down and unmoving a few feet away. Blood was seeping onto the tan carpet from where the bullet had exited the back of his head. "All I asked was for you to pay what you owe; instead, you chose to pay with your life."

King Dex tucked his weapon away and turned his back on the murder scene and left the room. He fixed the jacket on his tan Tom Ford suit and ran his hand over the deep waves in his low-cut hair. For a man in his forties, he knew he looked damned good, and he had chocolate skin that made women half his age sing his name. In the past, his sweet looks were what made his enemies count him out, but eventually, they learned just how ruthless he could be. He'd earned the name "King" a long time ago, and it was a title that he planned to keep for long time coming.

Next to the front door of the house, there was a suitcase waiting patiently for him. It contained the money he made Edward remove from a safe upstairs before he killed him— $50,000 to be exact. To a man of his stature that was a small amount of money; however, it was more of a respect thing for King Dex. If he let an ant steal a crumb of food from his camp, somebody would go unfed.

He couldn't have that, so he had to make an example out of Edward to anyone else who thought it would be funny to steal from him and make a profit.

He left the house and headed toward the black SUV waiting for him. The driver holding open the back door was wearing an all-black suit and sunglasses, although the sun had gone down hours before.

"Thank you, Lawson." King Dex nodded his head at the older gentleman and got inside of the car beside Dorian. "Who did you say has the other half of the one hundred thousand dollars Edward made off the original fifty?"

"His name is Rick Dumphy. They were partners, I guess."

"Find him."

"Already on it."

Once Lawson was back in the car, they drove away from the scene and, five minutes later, a white van arrived.

In hindsight, maybe moving out in such a hurry might not have been a good idea, but it was too late to turn back now. The night had come and gone, and when Ava woke up, she felt the cool, soft bed of the hotel underneath her body. She stirred slightly, not wanting to get up.

The first thing she did was check her phone, and she saw that she had fifteen missed calls from her mother. She was sure that Alaya wanted to apologize; and, while she knew that alcohol probably had a lot to do with her mother's behavior, she wasn't trying to hear that. Ava loved her mother with her entire heart, but she knew things between them would never be the same until she left Dumphy. He was just another no-good man who had landed on a gold mine, and there was no way that Ava could go back to that house. Her name was on the lease, and she needed to contact the landlord to see about getting her name removed. But, first, she needed to get up for wor—

"Shit!" Ava said, jumping up.

She finally took notice of the time on the phone and panicked. How could she have slept until one o'clock in the afternoon? She was supposed to be at work in thirty minutes, and all she could think about was the look on Amanda's face, telling her that the last time was her last time to be late.

She scrambled to find something to throw on from one of the bags on the side of the bed, and she silently thanked herself for having sense enough to take a shower the night before. She threw on a light pink blouse and a pair of socks, and she pulled up her jeans, hopping around the room to find her brown combat boots. She spotted them the moment she buttoned her jeans. She stuck her feet in them after she grabbed her purse and coat from the hotel room desk.

Ava ran out of the room, throwing many apologies over her shoulder after bumping into a few people staying on her floor. She didn't stop running until she was inside of her car and on her way to her job. She had about twenty minutes to get to work and, if traffic permitted, she could get there in fifteen.

It was just her luck that the cars on the streets cooperated with her need to rush, and she made it to her job at three minutes to her clock-in time. Ava was out of breath when she reached the employees' room, but she had no time to catch her breath because of the busy lunch hour.

"Girl, I thought I saw a ghost when you walked in!" Damien exclaimed and playfully swatted her on the arm as she picked up a tray of plates from the kitchen window.

"I'm going to be a ghost if you make me drop this food!" Ava grinned at him. "You know Amanda will have my ass if I mess up one more time in this joint!"

"Amanda, S'manda. Here, girl, let me help you," Damien said, grabbing a round tray and placing some of the plates on it.

"Thank you, baby," Ava said, feeling the relief once some of the weight was gone. "You're amazing!"

The two of them tackled the table of a big party that looked to be celebrating something. There were three couples, one of them obviously older than the other two, and six children. After they handed the food out, Damien made a quick getaway as Amanda made her way over to the table.

"What happened to our original server?" one of the older black men said. He reminded Ava of a pastor in a Nineties' black comedy movie. He had a head full of hair that had grays mixed in it and a beard that matched perfectly. His lips were large and took up his most of his face, and he was a bit on the heavyset side. Still, his voice was pleasant, and he didn't ask his question in a confrontational way.

"Yes," the woman sitting next to him said. Ava assumed she was his wife by the way she had her fork in his pork chops. "Where did she go? Her name was Katrina, I think."

"Honestly, I'm not sure." Ava offered up a kind smile. "But my name is Ava, and I'm going to be more than happy to take care of you folks tonight. Does your food look good, or is there anything I can take back for you?"

"Nope!" the man boomed. "Everything looks amazing so far. I love coming here, so since today is my fiftieth birthday, I couldn't think of no other place I'd rather be in all of Omaha, Nebraska!"

"Oh, my goodness!" Ava put her hand to her chest and winked at his wife. "You can't be fifty, young man! You don't look a day older than twenty-five!"

The entire family broke out in laughter, but the man looked to be pleased by Ava's comment. She learned a long time ago that the way to people's hearts and pockets was through kindness.

"Oooh, Grandma! I think she's flirting with Papa!" one of the older kids said and raised her eyebrow up at her grandmother.

"This child ain't crazy," the woman said and returned Ava's wink. "I think all of Nebraska knows about all the women I beat down over this man in my day!"

"And I don't want no part of that!" Ava joined in their laughter and playfully threw her hands in the air.

"Well, you listen, honey." The woman reached and grabbed Ava's hand. "Thank you for the food, and we'll call you if we need anything. I'm Tara Douglas, and this is my husband, Dan."

"Pleased to meet you, and I'll be over to check on you in a bit." Ava took her leave and went to check on her other tables; but, instead, she was met by Amanda.

"Were you on time today, Ava?" she asked, blocking Ava from going any farther.

"Yes, ma'am," Ava replied, wishing they were farther from the Douglases' table.

"Good, but I'll be sure to check your punch to validate your word."

"Okay," Ava said and tried to walk around her; but Amanda stopped her again.

"Your mother has been calling the restaurant nonstop looking for you. I thought you knew that the restaurant phone was not to be used for personal use."

"And that's why I have a cell phone," was Ava's response. She was starting to feel that Amanda was just looking for reasons to be upset with her. "She probably got the number from your Web site."

"Well, tell her to stop calling! You can talk to her when you're off at eleven tonight!"

"Eleven?" Ava raised her brows at Amanda. "I get off at nine tonight. My schedule has been the same since I started working here."

"Well, tonight I need you until eleven." Amanda cocked her head and faked a concerned expression. "Is that a problem for you? Because if it is, I'm sure there are other places hiring that will let you off at nine."

Before she could say another word, Amanda walked off, leaving Ava to choke on her words. Ava was certain that the Douglases had heard the exchange, but she didn't look back to see. Instead, she went to check on the other table like she was trying to do in the first place. Although she didn't have anything to do after work, she didn't like the way that Amanda had just come at her. It wasn't right and, when she signed on, Ava had agreed to a specific schedule. Maybe this was Amanda's way of punishing her for her tardiness. Either way, Ava was fuming.

"Damn, girl, what's got your panties so far up your ass right now?" Damien asked when she plopped down next to him in the employees' room.

Hours had gone by, and when it was finally time for her lunch break, she took her bad attitude with her. The only good thing so far about the night was that the Douglases gave her a hundred-dollar tip wrapped around a business card. She sighed and told Damien all about Amanda and that she was making her stay a few extra hours.

"That bitch!" Damien exclaimed since they were in the employees' room alone and able to talk freely. "What the fuck gives her the right to just randomly change your schedule?"

"Exactly." Ava shook her head. "I'm already dealing with enough, especially after last night."

"Hold on." Damien put his hands up and looked into Ava's face curiously. "What happened last night?"

"I went home to my mom having another wild party." Ava rolled her eyes. "We got into it pretty bad."

"Was it behind her boyfriend, Dopey?"

"Yes." Ava couldn't even muster up a smile at him purposely mispronouncing Dumphy's name. "I found out that the reason we were so behind on the light bill is because she'd been giving him all the money I give her."

"What!" His mouth fell open in disbelief. "Shut up. Girl, you are lyin'! Don't she know how hard you have to work for your money? Hell, look at what you had to deal with today with Amanda's punk ass."

"I know. That's why I packed my shit and left."

"You left?"

"Yup."

"Shut up! I thought your name was on the lease."

"It is, but I have to get my shit off now. Especially since she has a grown-ass man living there."

"I heard the fuck out of that. Where you been staying at? A hotel?" When Ava nodded her head, Damien shot her a look. "Girl, why the hell you in a hotel when you could have come to my house? You know my doors are open to you any time!"

"Boy, stop." Ava smiled. "If you weren't such a freak nasty thing I might have considered that. Ain't nobody trying to hear you bang your boo thang out every night."

Damien made the "Stevie J" face and blinked his eyelashes. "You right, you right!" Damien said and then laughed. "Daddy can't get enough of this, okay?"

By all means, Ava didn't care about the fact that Damien was gay. She'd even met his little friend a couple of times. Still, the last image she wanted in her mind was of her friend's sex life, no matter who he was bedding. She quickly decided to change the subject before Damien could tell her how much whipped cream he used the night before.

"Anywayysss, I'm just going to look for a little apartment. Just something I can afford for right now. I can't go back to that house because even if she gets rid of him—"

"She'll get a new man just like him."

"Exactly. So, let me go on ahead and boss my life up and get on my own two feet."

"And you will." Damien reached forward and touched her hand. "I'm here for you, sis, always."

Ava was not one who was prone to being affectionate, but she was touched by Damien's words. They continued to chat for a few more minutes before they checked the clock and saw that it was time to go back out on the floor. On their way out of the employees' room, two of the other servers, Drew and Brianna, came inside to take their break. Ava wanted to roll her eyes because that meant she and Damien would be on the floor by themselves. She was positive that both had already gone over their breaks, and she was surprised that Amanda wasn't on their necks. Ava understood that she wasn't anybody's parent, so questioning was, well, out of the question. Instead, she followed Damien and got back to the busy floor.

Ava should have prepared herself because she was met with pure chaos. The dining floor was crowded and noisy. Every table she passed had a request for her: more water, more napkins, or extra silverware. She felt like she was moving nonstop for the next few hours, and it was a good thing, because it kept her mind off reality.

After the lunch and evening rushes, the chaos died down and Ava could relax a little bit, until a group of people her age entered the restaurant. Those kinds of customers were usually her favorite. Although they didn't tip well, they often livened the place up a bit. Plus, she knew that sometimes a person just wanted to go out to eat and pay for their own food, not their server's bills. However, the group that had just walked in looked as if they could afford a tip and then some.

There were three girls and two boys. The girls all had designer Coach bags with matching boots. Two of the girls looked like sisters with their smooth cocoa skin and wide eyes. One of them rocked box braids while the other had her hair braided into a big bun on the top of her head. They both had makeup covering their faces, looking like they had just left a photo shoot, and their outfits screamed chic. One was taller than the other, and if they, in fact, were sisters, Ava assumed that she was the older of the two. The other girl, however, was the one who stood out. She was a pretty, yellow-skinned girl with naturally long, straight hair highlighted auburn. Her smile was enough to light up a room, and her cheekbones would make Halle Berry jealous. Her outfit was on point, too, from her bomber jacket all the way to her light jeans.

"Hey!" Ava greeted them as soon as they were seated. "My name is Ava Dunning, and I'm going to be the one helping you guys today. Can I start you off with some drinks and appetizers?"

"Can I just get, uhhh . . ." the darker of the two boys started while looking at the drink menu. "Let me just get a Pepsi, with lemon."

"What?" the tall girl asked and made a face at the boy's unusual request.

"Ay, look," the boy said and raised an eyebrow her way. "Don't judge it unless you try it!"

"You'd be surprised at how often I get that request," Ava said jokingly and jotted his drink order down in her notepad.

"See? Look, Nique, you got our waitress lookin' at me all funny and shit!"

"You did that to yourself, Blane." Nique shrugged and then turned back to Ava. "Me and my little sister will have a Sprite."

"I can order for myself, you know!" the girl who looked just like Nique said.

"What do you want to order then, Londa?" Nique asked, rolling her eyes; and Londa smirked.

"A Sprite."

"You get on my damn nerves!"

Ava smiled at their bickering and jotted the two Sprites down. The other guy sitting at the table was eyeing her up and down. She tried to ignore the look in his eyes when she focused her attention on him, but there was something about his slight smile that made her uneasy. He wasn't a bad-looking young man at all. He actually was very attractive, but he was definitely the type who knew it. Whereas Blane rocked shoulder-length dreads, this guy's hair was cut into a neat brush cut. He had no waves, but his line-up was so crisp, and it aligned perfectly with his beard. He wasn't brown-skinned, nor was he light-skinned. He was the color of a bronze peanut with eyes the color of mahogany. He licked his full lips, answering Ava's question before she even asked it.

"I'll take a lemonade, baby." He paused and then licked his lips again. "Unless you're on the menu. If so, I'll have that."

Ava didn't miss a beat. She was so used to men hitting on her because of the size of her breasts and round behind that rejecting men seemed like second nature to her. She wasn't rude about it at all, though. Instead, she shook her head and jotted his order down with a smile.

"No, I am not on the menu, but I'll bring your lemonade right out. I'll even make it strawberry with no upcharge, but only if you never use that pickup line again."

"Damn! That was the nicest curve I've ever heard in my life!" Blane said, wide-eyed and clutching the top of his head. He held the look of someone who had just witnessed history in person. "Yo, son! You can't even come back after that one, Vince!"

The entire table burst into laughter, and even Vince cracked a smile. She didn't know it yet, but Ava had sparked an interest in him. Whether that was a good or bad thing, only time would tell.

"Excuse my friends, Ava," the girl with the auburn hair finally spoke up. "They took some shots before we came out."

"Oh, really? Are you guys celebrating something?"

"Yeah: getting paid!" Londa said, running her hands through her box braids with one hand and high-fiving her sister with the other.

"Hell yeah!" Nique agreed with a grin.

"Y'all are so damn ghetto!"

"And you're not, Vy? Girl, bye. You the same bitch who keeps a flask of Henny in her purse. Designer bag or not, you ain't fooling nobody!"

Vy looked like she wanted to smack Nique but, instead, she looked over her shoulder real quick before pulling the flask from her purse. She took a shot and put it back like nothing had happened, and she looked up into Ava's grinning face.

"The hood will never leave me," Vy said, "but I don't go to nice places acting a damn fool like them. I'll just take a lemonade as well, regular for me. And can we start with Buffalo wings for an appetizer? You do have hot wings, right? My bad; I didn't even look at the menu."

"Yes, we do!" Ava nodded, scribbling in her notepad. "I'll go get that put in for your table and give you guys a few moments to look over the menus for entrees. How does that sound?"

"Good! Thank you, Ava."

Ava turned to go put in their appetizer and get their drinks. As she was walking, she heard Blane say, "I like her. She gon' get a fat-ass tip from me as long as the food good!"

She smiled to herself. Nothing made her feel better than knowing she was doing well at her job. She grabbed their drinks and took their orders.

At that time, there wasn't anyone else in her section, so she found herself lingering around their table once their food was brought out. Ava was what you would call a loner, but not by choice. She didn't really have time to make real friends or have fun because she was always working. It felt good to vibe out with people her age and act like a normal twenty-five-year-old woman. She clicked the most with Vy. Through conversation, she found out that Vy's father wasn't in her life either, and her mother was an alcoholic. She'd been on her own since she was eighteen and, from the looks of it, she was doing well for herself.

"I wish I could afford a bag like that or those boots, girl," Ava was saying as she wiped off a table next to theirs. "I feel like I'm just slaving for bills right now. And since I left home, I really have to penny-pinch."

She didn't know why she'd told Vy about the fact that she was living in a hotel until she found somewhere to stay, but she did. Words seemed to roll off both their tongues in their conversation. It was like they'd known each other for years.

"You're good at your job, like, really good," Vy said, smiling. "You probably get good tips."

"I do, but it's still not enough to really live how I want to. You know?"

At that moment, Ava's stomach growled so loud, and she was instantly embarrassed because everyone stopped eating. *Shit.* She wanted to kick herself. *Now they proba-bly think I'm broke and starving.*

"Damn, sis, are you hungry?" Londa asked; but, instead of laughing, her face held a serious expression. "We're all eating in front of you and shit. I feel rude."

"Yeah, man." Blane waved his hand at the hot wings and fries. "We barely touched those if you want some."

"Here," Vy said and cut a piece of her tender steak and scooped up some mashed potatoes with it. "Try this. It's a fire combination!"

"I can't," Ava said, shaking her head. "I'm not supposed to eat unless I'm on break."

"Girl, take a bite! You've been working hard all night. The least we can do is feed you. Here." Vy wasn't taking no for an answer.

She held the fork out to Ava, who scanned the dining floor for her boss. When she didn't see Amanda anywhere in sight, she took the fork from Vy and put the food in her mouth. It was delicious and, like Vy said, the flavor combination exploded in her mouth.

"Oh, my God," Ava moaned. "That shit is good."

"Here, eat some of these wings, too," Blane said again. "You can't say no if we're asking you to dine with us. The customer is always right."

"Nigga, this ain't no call center!" Nique laughed but pulled out a chair beside her.

Reluctantly, Ava sat in the open seat and continued to eat and talk to them. She stopped looking around for Amanda and just went on to enjoy herself. There wasn't anyone else in the restaurant at that point, and all of the tables were cleaned. She didn't see a reason why she couldn't eat and enjoy herself. She assumed that Amanda had left early the way she always did on the weekend, and Ava just knew she didn't have anything to worry about.

Before she knew it, so much time had gone by that it was time for the restaurant to close. She stood up to get their bill, but as soon as she turned her back to the table, she bumped chests with the person she assumed was gone.

"Amanda!"

"Shocked to see me?" Amanda raised one of her eyebrows at Ava's surprised expression. "Can I ask what exactly you are doing?"

"About to go get their bill." Ava motioned back to the table of watching eyes.

"But before that, I could have sworn I saw you dining with them."

"I—"

Amanda held her hand up, silencing Ava. "Is this what I pay you to do? To sit up here and lollygag? Didn't you already have a break?"

"Amanda, they asked me to sit with them."

"And I would assume that you would be smart enough to tell them no! Are you stupid like the rest of the people in this neighborhood? Do you just not care about your job?"

Ava bit her tongue, not wanting to say what was in her mind. Of course Amanda would compare her to the people in the neighborhood, assuming they were all lowlifes with nothing going for themselves. Of course this white woman would take a job as the manager in a hood spot and walk around as a superior being. Of course she would look down her nose at Ava and talk to her crazy because she knew she needed her job. So, instead of giving Amanda a piece of her mind, Ava just shook her head.

"I do care about my job, Amanda. I was on time to work today, and I made a killing on tips."

"So, this is how you get your tips? Flirting with both the men and the women? I saw you eat the food from that lady's fork, so don't try to deny it." Amanda's thin lip was turned up, and it seemed like she was getting a few things off her chest. "I've seen you leave this place with nearly three times as much in tips than the other waiters. What are you doing, screwing the customers? Like a whore? I've been trying to put up with your negligence since you started working here, but not anymore. You're fired!"

Ava's eyes enlarged, and she tried to make sense of what she had just heard. She couldn't believe it. She was the reason why most of the people even decided to come back to the restaurant, and it wasn't because she was "screwing" any of them. She couldn't afford to lose her job, especially now since she'd left home. The image of Dumphy's smug face haunted her thoughts, and Ava blinked it quickly away. She couldn't go back to that house, especially not without a job.

"No, Amanda, please. I need this job. I don't have anywhere to live right now, and I'm saving up for my own place."

"Looks like you better start job hunting then. Finish up and leave." Amanda went to turn her back on Ava, but a voice shocked them both.

"Yo, on the real, that ain't even cool!" Nique said. "She sat with us because we asked her to. Ain't no reason to fire the girl!"

"Well, I appreciate the concern, but Ava has been skating on thin ice for some time now. This is the best thing I can do for my restaurant."

"Didn't you just say she brings in more than all your other workers in tips? Sounds to me like she does a good-ass job." Vince mugged Amanda so hard that the fake smile she wore left her face. "And by the good service she gave us, I can guarantee you that she isn't fuckin' none of the niggas who come in here."

"I hate white bitches like this, man," Londa said, pushing her plate forward. "Come to the hood and just look down on us like we ain't shit. It probably felt good saying that, huh? 'You're fired!' Yo, Vince, do it!"

Vince made a face and mimicked Amanda's when she fired Ava. The table laughed again, and Ava couldn't help but crack a smile at how red Amanda's face was turning. She opened her mouth to speak, but Vy interrupted her by jumping to her feet.

"We're leaving now, Ava. No need for you to get our bill. I ain't paying for shit."

"You probably couldn't afford the meal anyway," Amanda couldn't help but say as the others followed suit.

On cue, Vince and Blane pulled out rolls of hundred-dollar bills and flashed them for everyone to see. Ava had never seen anyone with that much money in their pockets, and it was clear that they could afford any meal they decided to sit down and eat. They said nothing else; instead, they put the money back and headed for the front door of the restaurant. Nique and Londa followed close behind, but not before rolling their eyes at Amanda. Vy gathered up her things and made to leave with the others, but not before she stopped like she was waiting for something.

"You coming?" Vy looked over her shoulder into Ava's stunned eyes.

"Me?"

"Yes, you. Shit, you don't have a job anymore. Come have some fun with us."

Ava looked to the dirty table that still needed to be cleaned and then back to Amanda's angry face. She almost told Vy that no, thanks, she needed to stay and beg Amanda to keep her job. But then she replayed Amanda's words in her head and took her apron off.

"Good-bye, Amanda."

Ava threw her apron at Amanda's feet and followed quickly after Vy, leaving her old boss in her dust.

Not only did they all have money, but they drove nice cars, too. In the parking lot, Vince, Blane, and the girls got into a gold 2017 Chrysler 300 while Vy walked casually over to an all-black 2017 Chevy Impala. Vy's car made Ava's Impala look like the annoying little sister who wanted to tag along everywhere.

"That's your ride?" Vy said, pointing, and Ava nodded her head. "A'ight, hop in and we gon' follow you to wherever you're staying right now. You rolling with us tonight. You got something to wear tonight?"

Ava thought about her wardrobe, and her mind went to the dresses she wore when she went out. She'd worn all of them a number of times, and the one that could be a maybe, she knew, wouldn't have anything on whatever Vy was going to wear. Vy must have read Ava's face because she waved her hand in a "forget it" manner.

"Just follow me to my spot. I'll hook you up with something."

"Okay," Ava said and smiled in relief. She was glad Vy wouldn't have to see that she was staying in a hotel or the fact that all of her belongings could fit in three garbage bags.

She got in her car and waited for them to pull out first to follow them. She drove behind them and tried not to lose sight of their vehicles. It was a hard task to do, especially with everyone around her driving crazy, probably trying to make it to the club. The way Vy and them were driving, it was apparent that wherever they were taking her was out in West Omaha.

When they turned into the driveway of a home in a neighborhood off of 108th and Fort, Ava figured she was in the wrong place. The house was a ranch style with a two-car garage. Even in the dim light provided by the streetlights, she was blown away by how beautiful the house was. She couldn't tell if it was white or a very light blue, and she admired the white brick on the perimeter of the garage. The other two cars parked in the driveway and Ava parked hers on the street. Hesitant to get out of the car, she waited for them to do so first, which they did immediately.

"Come on, girl!" Nique waved Ava up to the front door of the house. "These white people out here ain't gon' fuck with you."

Ava looked around the quaint neighborhood and couldn't help but wonder what they were doing there. When she saw Vy unlock the door with a key, Ava assumed that it must be her parents' home. Reluctantly doing what Nique said, Ava once again followed them.

When she walked through the wide hallway, she was instantly blown away by the rest of the house. All of the walls in the home were snow white, and the carpet was a light beige color. To the right was a large kitchen with a three-seat marble island and all stainless-steel appliances. The floor was a dark wood that looked to have just been waxed. The dining room was a nice size and was connected to a big living room area that looked like it had never been sat in. There wasn't even a TV, just suede furniture and a décor that matched the kitchen floor.

She didn't notice until then that she passed the bedroom at the front of the house and there was another, the master, closer to the back and down another hallway. Everybody except Ava and Vy headed to the basement stairs, and Ava's feet wanted badly to trail behind just to see what was down there, but she fought her urges.

"My room is this way," Vy spoke to Ava, pointing to the room down the hallway. "Come on so you can check out my closet and find something for tonight. I heard that new club is supposed to be popping."

"Okay."

Before she knew it, Ava was in the biggest bedroom she'd ever seen in her life. Vy had a few portraits of herself hanging up on the walls, along with some frames that had pictures of her family. Well, Ava figured they were her family. She couldn't help but walk around the room and examine every inch. Not only did Vy have a California king-sized bed, but she had a luxurious bathroom and a walk-in closet. Ava's hands trailed the rim of Vy's long dresser that was below the mounted sixty-inch flat screen as she made her way back to the closet.

"This would be cute on you!" Vy said, completely missing the expression on Ava's face. "What you think?"

She was holding up a sleek nude dress that still had the tag on it. When Ava's eyes brushed over the price of the dress, she shook her head. "I can't pop the tag on a thousand-dollar dress!"

"Girl!" Vy shot her a fake annoyed look. "If you don't stop and try this damn dress on . . . I already know what I'm wearing, and the girls are probably downstairs getting ready as we speak."

"Are you sure?" Ava asked, taking the dress. She had to admit, the little off-the-shoulder, crossed-back dress was hot. It had been so long since she had been able to go shopping for herself, so she was excited at the fabric in her hand. She pressed it to her body and looked at herself in Vy's full-body mirror at the back of the closet. The dress went past her knees, but Ava knew that once her curves filled it out, it would stop a little past her thighs.

"Yes, I'm sure! Now choose what shoes you want to wear. Oooh!" Vy threw her hands in the air, as she had just had a stroke of genius. "I just got these bad-ass thigh-high red boots that would look amazing with that dress. Over there! Here, try these on with the dress."

Vy found the shoebox, handed it to Ava, and ushered her into the bathroom. Ava took one look at the dress and the shoes and already knew that they were a go. Instead of just trying them on, she decided that she might as well just get dressed.

In the closet, she found towels; and she hopped in the shower. She vigorously scrubbed the smell of grease from her body and found some shampoo in the shower to wash her hair with. All in all, it took Ava about thirty minutes to get ready; and when she stepped out of the bathroom, she felt like a new woman.

"Okayyy, li'l Ava with the good hair!" Vy said when she saw Ava standing there dressed. "I knew that dress would look good on you! And the bun in your hair goes well with the whole outfit, but—"

"But what?"

"I have this banging-ass wig that would look even better!"

"Oh no, I don't wear weaves like that."

"Girl, if you don't loosen up . . . Niggas love fake shit."

"So why aren't you wearing a weave then?"

"Because I just paid sixty dollars for this silk press, that's why! Now sit on the bed so I can grab this wig."

Vy disappeared for a few seconds and came back holding a jet-black bob wig. She took the bun out of Ava's hair, braided it into two French braids, and put a tight cap over them. Once she put the wig on, Vy ran and got her makeup bag so that she could beat Ava's face to the gods.

"Okay, bend your head a little. Yeah, just like th . . . Perfect! Go look at yourself. Girl, you bad!"

Reluctantly, Ava stood up and walked back into the bathroom to look at the catastrophe on her head. When she saw herself, a small gasp left her mouth. The blunt-cut bob with Chinese bangs, mixed with the edgy earth-tone makeup, made her look like a brand-new woman in a very good way.

"Wow," she said to herself, eyeing the sexy red lipstick that had found a home on her plump lips. "I look so—"

"Hot!" Vy burst out, coming up from behind her. "You can't lie. Ya girl got some skills!"

"Thank you," Ava said, smiling at her reflection.

"Well, you can't be the only one looking good. I'm about to hop in the shower too. Go look at some accessories in my jewelry box on my dresser and see if there's any that you want to wear."

Vy kicked Ava out of the bathroom, and soon water from the shower could be heard running. Ava found herself in front of Vy's jewelry box, and she felt like she was in a jewelry store. Everything looked so expensive, and although she wanted to lace herself out in diamonds, she settled on a thin gold rope chain and some gold stud earrings.

When Vy was done, she came out wearing nothing but a red thong and a strapless red bra. Her eyes instantly went to Ava's choice of jewelry, and she paused, placing her hand on her hip. "Girl, if you don't take that baby-ass necklace off and put on them diamonds . . ."

"They just look so expensive, Vy."

"They are, and it's a shame that they don't get worn more often. Look, Ava." Vy paused so she could go and grab the little black dress that she was wearing that night. She pulled it over her head and adjusted the spaghetti straps. Ava noticed that the back was completely open. "I know we just met and all, but I don't invite just anybody to come back to my crib, you feel me? I don't let just anybody come into my circle, so since you're here, understand that my shit is your shit. Okay?"

Ava didn't know why Vy was being so nice to her, but she felt that it was genuine. After only a few hours, Vy seemed to be one of the most solid people she'd met in a long time. She didn't argue; she just took off the necklace and earrings she currently had on and draped herself in the thick diamond necklace she wanted to wear originally. In her ears, she still wore studs, except they were big square-cut diamonds.

"Look at you, shinin' nigga!" Vy giggled as she touched up her hair with her flat iron. "Okay, let me put my heels on and we're out of here!"

Chapter 3

"Lay Lay! Get on in here, girl," a very tipsy Dumphy called from his girlfriend's bedroom. He'd gotten to her house an hour prior and was wondering why she hadn't come to join him in the room to sip on the Hennessy he had. It was late in the evening, but he was still in the day's clothes and shoes. His legs were sprawled out on the bed, and his erection was standing at attention. He wanted to feel her mouth wrap around his shaft and watch her pretty face swallow him whole. There were also a few things that he wanted to do to her, but she was somewhere moping around the house.

"Lay Lay!" he called again.

"What?" Lay Lay said, finally making her way to the bedroom. She was wearing a peach and white T-shirt and shorts pajama set with her hair tied up in a scarf. She cut her eyes at the man in her bed and put her hand on her hip. "Why do you keep hollering my name?"

"Because I want you to come give me some of that good lovin'!" he said, giving her a sly smile. "Come on over here, girl, and let me do some thangs to ya."

Lay Lay rolled her eyes and shook her head. The entire room smelled like alcohol, and she could tell that he hadn't taken a shower. The last thing she wanted to do was put her mouth on a dirty man, and she let him know that.

"Dumphy, get up out of my bed with those dirty clothes on. I just washed the covers yesterday! And if you want me to do anything to you, you could at least have the decency to be clean. What kind of a woman do you think I am?"

Before she could hear his answer, she left the room again, going back to the wine she was sipping in the kitchen. Her mind was clouded, and she just wanted to be alone right then, but of course, that was too much like right for Dumphy. He followed right after her and was on her heels in seconds. He tried to grab her arm, but she snatched away and took her seat at the kitchen table.

"You still mad because your grown-ass daughter finally moved out? Is that why I can't get no pussy?"

"You can't get no pussy because I'm not letting no dirty-dick-ass man run up in me! Now please, go shower or something. I just want to be left alone."

"Nah." Dumphy shook his head and slammed the fifth of Hennessy he had in his hand down on the wooden table. "This is about that little bitch! Ever since she walked out of here, you've been in this funky-ass mood!"

"Well, you didn't have to talk to her like that!" Lay Lay finally shouted what she'd been thinking. "And don't call my daughter a bitch!"

When Ava first packed her things and drove off, Lay Lay only let her go because she was sure her baby girl would come home the next day. Well, she didn't; and Lay Lay hadn't received so much as a phone call. The more and more she thought about it, Ava had been right, and as she looked at Dumphy standing before her, all she saw was a sorry excuse for a man. She was ashamed that she had put him above the one person in the world who truly cared about her. "She is my daughter, and all you've done is disrespect her in her own home!" Lay Lay was suddenly boiling. "And how the hell do you have money for alcohol but 'that little bitch,' as you called her, was the one who had to pay the light bill? How do you have a fuckin' bottle of Hennessy, but you couldn't pay your car note?"

"Who the hell are you talkin' to, bitch?" Dumphy asked, towering over her in a threatening stance.

"You!" Lay Lay growled, standing back to her feet. She wrapped her skinny fingers around the wine bottle and prepared to use it if she had to. "I was going to tell you to give me my money back, but you know what? I just want you out of my damn house. Get out before I call the police on your dirty, no-good ass. Get all your shit and go!"

Dumphy looked at her dumbfounded, and without moving right away. He glared at her and contemplated his next move. The alcohol coursing through his system was screaming for him to knock her head off her shoulders, but that would have been a bad move on his part. She'd said one word, though, that seemed to sober him up a bit: police.

"You're gonna regret this," he said finally and stepped away from her.

Angrily, he went back to the bedroom so that he could get his duffle bag from the highest shelf in her closet. He stuffed all that he could into it and figured that she could do what she wanted with the rest. He could buy himself some new things with all the money he had now.

After the bag was securely shut and on his shoulder, he headed to the front door of the house. Lay Lay followed close behind him as he trudged down the stairs, and she waited for him to twist the knob.

"And don't come back, you sorry motherfucka!" she said as he swung the door open with force.

"Don't worry, he won't."

The voice caught Lay Lay by surprise because it was one that she didn't recognize. Standing on her doorstep were two men she'd never seen in her life. One was just under six feet tall, muscular, and dressed trendy like the kids Ava's age; and one was short, big, and bulky. They both had backpacks on, and their faces held the same distasteful expression at the sight of Dumphy. Lay Lay could tell he knew who they were by the sudden fear that washed over his face, but it didn't register with her that they were very bad people. All she wanted was for Dumphy to get out so she could get back to her Moscato, and when she spoke, attitude drenched her voice. "And who are you?"

"How rude of me," the man said. "Let me introduce myself. I am Dorian, and my big friend here is Preston. We were just about to knock on your door, but it seems that you brought us who we were looking for. What's up, Dumphy? Long time no see."

His eyes pierced into Dumphy's, and the fire burning in them made it obvious that he hadn't come in peace. Whatever it was that Dumphy had gotten himself into, Lay Lay wanted no part of it.

"Dorian!" Dumphy stuttered. "What's good, my man? I was just on my way to King Dex's now. I have some things that I need to explain to him."

"Hmm, is that right?" Dorian asked, sucking his teeth and then looking to the man beside him. "I could have sworn we just heard his woman about to put him out. Or are my ears going bad?"

"Nah, boss." Preston's voice came out as a wheeze, most likely because he was so fat. "That's what I heard too."

"I thought so." Dorian turned back to Dumphy. "I don't like when people lie to me. You were close with a man named Edward Franklin, correct? He's swimming with the fishes now. King Dex doesn't take kindly to people stealing from him. Where is the fifty thousand dollars?"

Dumphy hadn't talked to his old friend for a few days, but now he knew why. At first, anger set in because Edward was the one who had access to the money and he never told Dumphy how to get it. But then terror hit him, and he wondered how Dorian and his henchman were able to track him down. Somebody must have talked and told them where he was. He tried to take a step back into the house, but Lay Lay's palms pushing on his back stopped him.

"Dumphy, whatever you have going on, you need to do it away from here," Lay Lay said. "All of you, get the hell away from my house."

"I'm afraid we can't do that," Dorian said and brandished a silver 9 mm pistol from his waist. He waved it toward the door, motioning for them to get back inside of the house. "Not until one of you tells me where the money is."

Lay Lay gasped, and her heart instantly dropped to the pit of her stomach. "Dumphy, tell him where the money is." Lay Lay grabbed Dumphy's arm and shook him violently. The sight of the gun had terrified her, and something inside told her that it had been used many times before. When he said nothing, she shook him even harder. "Dumphy, tell him where the money is, you son of a bitch!"

"I don't know where it is," Dumphy said, moving his head from side to side. "Edward never told me."

"I think you do know where it is, but you just don't want to tell me." Dorian nodded his head at Preston, giving him a silent signal. "I, however, think I can get the information up out of you."

Before Lay Lay could scream and signal to one of her neighbors to call the police, she was getting thrown back inside of her house. Dumphy flew back too, and then Dorian stepped in, shutting the door behind him.

"It's such a shame that you got such a beautiful woman tied up in your mess," Dorian said, kneeling and stroking the side of Lay Lay's smooth face. "Now she has to pay too. Take her upstairs, Preston. Preferably to a place where there is no carpet. Things may get a little messy."

With mighty hands, Preston grabbed Lay Lay's hair and head scarf as well as her upper arm so that he could drag her up the stairs. When she began to scream and try to twist away from him, he shook her violently and punched her hard in the face.

"Shut up, bitch!" he said and hit her again. Blood leaked from her nose, and both of her lips were busted. He went to hit her again, but Dorian's voice stopped him.

"Enough," Dorian told him with a raised eye. "We still need her coherent."

"My bad, boss," Preston said. "My baby moms been tripping on me lately. I just needed a release of frustration."

"Well, take it out on this piece of shit then," Dorian said, kicking Dumphy, who was curled up at his feet, in the ribs. "Tie them up. I have a feeling this is going to be a long, bloody night."

Chapter 4

The night was going better than Ava could have ever expected. It had been so long since she was able to just let loose, and it felt good. Vy opened a tab for the two of them, and Ava was feeling like she was on cloud nine. She danced the night away in the dark club and let the waves coming from the loud speakers direct her body. It seemed as if the entire club had come together in one big party. There were no girls hating on the next, nor was there any beef between the men. Everything was just—

"Lit!" Blane yelled, coming over to join Ava and Vy on the dance floor. In his hand, he had an open bottle of champagne, and he poured swigs into both of their mouths before he too drank some more. "This club is live as hell, boy! All the fine bitches are out tonight!"

"Keep fuckin' with them 'bitches' and you're going to end up with fleas!" Vy shouted over the music.

"I ain't got none yet! So fuck it!"

Vy rolled her eyes at him and turned to Ava, who was still dancing. "Girl, I have to use the bathroom. Make sure this fool doesn't do anything stupid. The last time we went out, he tried to push up on a chick while her man was standing right beside her. I'm not trying to fight the whole club again behind his thirstiness!"

"Yeah, yeah, whatever. The bitch was lookin' like a snack, and I like snacks!" he said, winking.

When Vy walked away, Ava was left standing next to a prowling Blane. She watched him crash and burn as he tried to get the attention of several of the girls who walked by them. Although he had terrible pickup lines, she had to give him props for his relentlessness. After a pretty, chocolate girl mean-mugged him for commenting on her body, Ava had finally had enough.

"What are you doing?"

"What do you mean what am I doing? I'm choosing!" He added a little dance with his last word.

"Blane." She paused to laugh but quickly regained her wits. "Blane! You have some of the corniest pickup lines I have ever heard. You remind me of that one creepy uncle at a black barbecue. I heard you tell a girl, 'You remind me of my favorite gum: chewable!'"

"You didn't like that?" Blane put a hand on his chest and pretended to be offended. "That's one of my best lines, girl!"

"That might have worked in the Eighties, but this ain't the Eighties! These are grown-ass 'half woke' women. They appreciate a man with intellect. So, try a different approach."

"Like?"

"Like complimenting her outfit without mentioning her body. Or go out to the dance floor and start fucking it up! Girls love men who can dance and know how to have a good time. Stop going to them, and let them gravitate to you."

The moment the words left her mouth, Lil Uzi Vert's song "Money Longer" began blasting through the speakers of the club. It must have been Blane's song, because within seconds he was gone and in the middle of the dance floor. She watched him turn the whole club up with his dance moves, and she was about to go out there and join him, but a voice stopped her.

"You a counselor or something?"

Ava turned around and found herself looking up into the most complex set of brown eyes. They were beautiful, but their gaze intimidated her. They belonged to a smooth, chocolate-skinned man who towered over her like a basketball player. He had to be at least six feet tall, and he wore his hair cut in a short, tapered fade. His jawbone was square, but she could tell that with a full-on smile he would have defined cheekbones. His full lips curved slightly as he watched her study him, and she wanted to answer him, but she wasn't done admiring his body. He was outfitted in simple clothing: a pair of Levi's, a white Ralph Lauren T-shirt with a red Polo logo, and a fresh pair of Chicago 13s.

"No, I'm not a counselor," she said finally. "But, you're fine as hell so, if you want, I can counsel you." She usually wasn't that forward, but the liquor gave her a dose of liquid courage that she would never have had if she were sober. She gazed at him with bedroom eyes and returned his small smirk.

"Thank you." He responded to her fearlessness with a chuckle. "I appreciate the compliment."

"You're welcome . . ."

"Glizzy," he answered.

"Glizzy?" she repeated out loud, trying to figure out why his name sounded so familiar. When she couldn't put a finger on it, she pushed the sounding bell to the back of her mind. "Nice to meet you. I'm . . . I'm Cinderella."

She wasn't sure why she said that, and the look on his face showed that he was just as confused as she was inwardly.

"Cinderella?"

"Yes." She winked at him. "By the end of the night, if I still like you, I'll tell you my real name."

"Well, Cinderella, have a drink with me."

It wasn't a question; it was a request to which Ava had no objection. He took her soft hand in his and led her to the bar, where he ordered them a few shots of tequila. Ava was already on her level and, after they took the first shot, he gave the other two to a couple sitting at the bar beside them.

"What did you do that for?" Ava asked, slightly upset. "You think I can't handle my liquor?"

"Chill. I didn't say all that," he said and then turned his head with a smile. "But you are pretty fucked up right now."

Ava's laugh came from her belly and left her mouth. She playfully swatted Glizzy on the arm and shook her head. "You're right. I am really fucked up right now. I've been mixing dark with light all night like a damn fool."

"Never a fool, mama; just a woman looking to have a good time. Ain't nothing wrong with that."

"Well, that's the truth. I had a long week," she said, not knowing why she was being so loose at the lips. Everything was just weighing on her shoulders, and she needed an outlet badly. "I really needed this."

She spotted Vy a ways away on the dance floor with Londa and Nique. When Vy finally looked Ava's way, instantly her eyes went to Glizzy and then to Ava. She raised her eyebrow and mouthed, "What's going on?" Before Ava could mouth anything back, Glizzy's Southern accent sounded in her ear.

"If you need to be drunk to balance out your lows then, I agree, it must have been one hell of a week. Tell me about it."

"You don't really want to know. You're just asking to be nice. We can talk about something else. Like where you're from. That isn't a Nebraskan accent you have."

"You're right, it's not. I'm from Houston. I just moved out here last year to be closer to my father. That's not what we were talkin' about, though. I understand we just met, but one thing you need to know about me is that I don't ask questions I don't want to know the answer to. Now, speak up."

There was something about his demanding demeanor that turned Ava on. His eyes were locked on hers, and the look on his face was genuine. Maybe he wasn't faking the funk. A man like him didn't need to lie to kick it. He was so fine that with a simple hello he could take home any woman in that club.

"Okay." She sighed. "Well, first, my mom and I had an argument. She has this boyfriend, and he just uses her. He doesn't pay any of the bills, and I kept having to pick up their slack. It was just too much, and that last fight was the worst. I packed all my shit and left. Haven't talked to her since."

"Okay, and what else?"

"How do you know there is something else?"

"Because we all fight with our parents. That ain't nothing to really sweat. That's your mom. She is never going to just turn her back on you, even if you do feel like she's putting her man over you right now. She'll come around. Don't even trip off of that. Now, what else is weighing on your brain?"

She thought about telling him that she'd lost her job earlier that day, but she changed her mind at the last minute. She didn't want him to know that she was staying in a hotel and that she didn't have a clue what she was going to do about money now. No. She didn't want the image, whatever image, he had of her to be tainted by a woman who needed a handout. So, instead, she shook her head and shrugged her shoulders.

"That was it. We just have never fought like that before." She averted her eyes back to the dance floor.

She wasn't a good liar, and it was obvious that Glizzy didn't believe a word she said, but he didn't press her. "Yeah, a'ight. Whatever you say," he said and grabbed her hand to force her to face him. "Dance with me."

"What?"

"We don't have much time left to get lost in each other, and I really would like to know your name. So, will you dance with me?"

"Lead the way, Prince Charming."

Ava and Glizzy made their way to the middle of the dance floor. It was like the area they chose instantly cleared, and the only two who mattered were them. They danced to the sound of Trey Songz's voice, and whenever she tried to push away from him, he pulled her back.

"Why do you keep running from me?" he asked with his lips to her ear.

"I don't know. I don't remember the last time I did this."

"Did what, dance?"

"No, this. Felt this feeling in the pit of my stomach. I don't even know you."

"Maybe in another life our souls touched." He stroked her cheek with his finger. "Or maybe it's just the alcohol."

"Maybe."

They were pressed so closely together that there wasn't even room for air to get through. There was no way for her to evade his charm; he was truly a prince of it. Ava was beyond mesmerized, and she couldn't hear the music being played anymore. Their bodies had stopped moving, but their eyes still danced. Without even thinking about it, Ava stood on her tiptoes and leaned into him until their lips met like old friends. His matched the softness of hers, and they melted into each other. She didn't care about who might have been watching them; she was too focused on Glizzy's tongue in her mouth. She didn't know how long they had been kissing, but the sound of multiple gunshots broke them abruptly apart.

"Get the prince!" she heard someone say, and before she knew it, Glizzy was ripped from her grasp, leaving her alone in a sea of panicked people. She felt her body being jerked in every direction as people rushed to get past her.

"Cinderella!"

She heard Glizzy call for her over the commotion. She tried to locate him by the direction of his voice, and she found him close to the entrance of the club. He was reaching for her while fighting against two big, burly men trying to get him out of the door. She started toward him, but more gunfire rang out, and instinct told her to drop to the floor.

"Ahh!" she called out when a girl who had to weigh at least 180 pounds fell on her leg. Ava tried to push the girl off, but she seemed to be too scared to move. The way the girl was lying and the fact that the club was still dark caused others to trip over her. Ava tried her best to free herself, but she just wasn't strong enough.

"Get the fuck off of me!" she screamed as fear set in. She didn't want to die.

Just as she was about to kick the girl in the head with her free foot, she felt two strong sets of hands grab both of her arms.

"We got you, baby girl," Vince said as he and Blane pulled her free.

In the process, Ava's right boot came off, but she didn't even care to grab it. She just wanted to be as far away from the warzone as possible. She ran out of the club awkwardly behind them, ignoring the pain in her ankle.

"Where's Vy?" she asked as they burst through the doors.

"Right there." Blane pointed to Vy's car, which was parked right outside the entrance.

He opened the door for her and made sure that she was safely inside before slamming the door shut and patting the top of the car, giving Vy the okay to pull off. She did so with no hesitation. The club had started to swarm with red and blue flashing lights. When they drove through the parking lot, Ava couldn't help but try to make out Glizzy in the crowd. Maybe he had waited for her. When she didn't see him, she shook her head at her silliness. Of course he hadn't waited. Why would he care if she was safe?

"Fuck!" Vy yelled, making Ava jump in her seat. When she saw that she had startled her friend, she put her head back and looked at the roof of the car. "My bad, girl. I just get so irritated when motherfuckas can't just go out and have a good time. I see enough dead bodies as it is. The last thing I want is to see one when I'm off the fucking clock."

Ava tried to comprehend Vy's words, but there was no underlying meaning that she could find. Her heart froze over and, in that moment, it came to light that she didn't even really know Vy, or the others for that matter. They just seemed like cool people to her, and she needed to get away. But right then she began thinking and trying to put a few puzzle pieces together. Vy had just said she saw dead bodies on a regular basis. She drove a nice car and lived in a house that most adults couldn't afford. What did she have to do to get that kind of money?

"Oh, my God. You're a murderer." Ava's hand clamped over her mouth as the words slipped out. She didn't mean to say them out loud, but it was too late. The cat was out of the bag.

"A murderer?" Vy said and looked at Ava like she was simple. "I ain't never caught a body in my life, but don't mistake that with the thought that I wouldn't do what I had to do if the situation called for it."

"How do you get all of your money? I mean, how can you afford this car and the house you live in? Where do you work and what do you do?"

The light turned green, but Vy didn't go. Instead, she stared at Ava as if she was trying to make a big decision. The cars behind them went around her because she stayed planted and, before they knew it, the light was red again. When she finally opened her mouth to say out loud whatever it was that she was contemplating, her phone began ringing loudly in the cup holder.

"Yeah?" she answered and paused so whoever was on the other end could speak. "Right now? I'm still in my club clothes." She paused again. "Yeah, she's still with me." Pause. "Okay, bring two sets of everything and I'm on my way. Send the address to my burner."

When she hung up, she clenched her eyes shut and gripped the steering wheel.

"What's wrong?" Ava asked, noticing the change in her demeanor.

"You need a job, right?" Vy asked, and Ava nodded her head slowly. "Well, you're about to see exactly what I do and maybe get paid in the process."

Vy hit a wild U-turn the moment the light turned green again, and she sped off in the other direction.

Chapter 5

Ava didn't know what she was getting herself into when she nodded her head, but she would soon find out. Instead of taking her back to the house, Vy pulled up to an abandoned warehouse in the middle of nowhere. There, Ava was able to make out the two cars that Blane, Vince, Nique, and Londa had been in. There also was an all-white van that Ava had never seen before. Vy hurried to park and jumped out of the vehicle as soon as the key was out of the ignition. Ava, not wanting to be left alone in the dark parking lot, hopped out right behind her. The concrete was cold under her one bare foot. She almost forgot that she'd left her shoe behind at the club.

"Vy, what are we doing here?" Ava asked when she caught up.

Vy ignored her and continued into the building with Ava fresh on her heels. The others were already there, and Ava was bewildered at what they were doing. Although the building was seemingly abandoned, the lights worked, and the air was cool like the AC was on. All the walls of the rooms that had once been inside were torn down, leaving a completely open space. She could hear the echo of the old pipes in the building dripping water on the ground, and a strong smell of musk invaded her nostrils.

While she was busy taking in her surroundings, the others were bustling around one of the two long tables there. They all seemed to be moving in a hurry, stuffing things from the table into the bags on their backs.

Ava also took notice that none of them were in their club clothes anymore. Instead, they wore less flattering sleek white jumpsuits and gray shoes like the ones employees wore in fast-food restaurants. The main thing that caught her eyes was that one of the two tables was completely covered with firearms. Ava had never seen so many guns up close in real life. They ranged from handguns to automatics, and her heart began to beat like a drill team at a parade.

"Vy," Ava started, beginning to pose her question again, but Vy was too busy stripping her clothes from her body. "Vy, what we doing here? Why are there guns?"

When Vy didn't answer, Blane threw a jumpsuit Ava's way. Ava caught it and held it up in the air, not knowing what she was going to do with it.

"We don't have time for you to just stand there staring at it. Put it on," Blane instructed. "Your shoes are over there."

Ava was still stunned and watched Vy switch into her own jumpsuit. She then grabbed two backpacks by Blane and began loading them with the heavy-duty cleaning supplies that were on the table that everyone was standing around. Nique and Londa finished loading their backpacks first and went over to the gun table. Their hands wrapped around their weapons of choice, and it was obvious to Ava that it wasn't their first rodeo. The boys followed and, soon after, Vy did too. When she finally looked up at Ava, she saw that she was still standing frozen in place.

"You said you wanted to know how I get all my money, right? If you want to make a quick five stacks, I suggest you put that jumpsuit on. Otherwise, you're going to be left waiting here until we come back."

Ava had so many questions about what was going on around her, but by the way everyone was rushing, she knew she wouldn't get the answers she was looking for. Nobody was waiting around to see what her next move was; they were focused on their own. Her mind was beating her head up trying to figure out what in the world they did to need that much firepower.

She was scared, and she suddenly regretted coming with Vy in the first place. Her life was in shambles. The last thing she needed to do was go to jail behind people she barely even knew. But, still, $5,000 sounded really good to her. She needed that kind of money in her life, especially since she was now jobless. Her arms and hands moved before they were even commanded to.

Vy was the only one paying attention as Ava undressed and put the jumpsuit on. When she was done, Vy handed her a pair of the gray shoes, socks, and a backpack.

"Go grab a gun," she said. When she saw Ava hesitate, she went and placed her hands on her shoulders. "Trust us, we got you. We don't let just anyone in this circle. Ain't nobody got no complaints with you being here, so that means you're one of us. Let's get this money. Blane!"

"What's good?"

"Grab me that Glock 20 for Ava."

"You sure? That's a big body, Vy. She don't even look like she's shot a BB gun a day in her life."

"Just get me the gun, Blane."

He shot her a look but did as he was told. When he handed Ava the gun, he showed her how to wrap her hand around the trigger.

"I doubt you'll have to use this tonight, but if you do, I suggest that you shoot with two hands. If you aren't used to the power, this motherfucka will knock you back. You feelin' me?"

Ava nodded her head, although she wasn't. It was all like something out of a movie, something she never thought could be experienced in real life. She was in

Omaha, Nebraska for crying out loud. Most people thought the state consisted of cornfields, but there she was staring at a 10 mm in her hand.

"All right, we're ready! Let's go before we lose out on this money. The last thing we need is King Dex on our necks about not holding up our end of the contract."

Londa's voice echoed in the building, and everyone headed out of the building toward the white van. Outside, Ava walked slowly behind them, mentally telling herself that she didn't have to do anything she didn't want to do.

Vince took notice of this, and while everyone was hopping inside of the vehicle, he touched Ava's arm softly. "Listen, not everything in the world is glitter or gold. Shit in real life isn't like the Huxtables. In order for some of us to live the good life, we have to get our hands dirty. Vy fucks with you tough, for some reason, and she usually doesn't like anybody. She is trying to look out for your pockets, and trust me, all this isn't as bad as it looks," he told her. "Since I've been working for King Dex, I have never had to pull a trigger. It's an easy job, and I know you need the Bens. Just do what we tell you to do and get paid. We got your back."

There was something about his words that soothed her. That was the second time in a day that somebody told her that they had her back. She thought back to the club incident and how they had all come back for her. She'd heard a long time ago that history wasn't the foundation of a friendship; it was all about the vibe. And, as crazy as it sounded, she felt a better vibe around them than she did when she was around her own mother. He held his hand out to help her step up into the van, and she made to grab it but paused.

"Before I get in this car, Vy said that you all aren't murderers. Yet we all have guns. What is it that you all do?"

Vince smiled and shrugged his shoulders slightly.

"We're cleaners."

***

Nique drove the van while the others sat in complete silence. The route she took was one that was all too familiar to Ava, being that it was the way she took every day to get home. She knew when they drove by Mrs. Hancock's house that they must be heading somewhere near her mother's house. She took in all the beautiful landscaping in her mother's neighbors' front yards because they were even more beautiful at night. As the van prepared to pass the home she had left, Ava couldn't help but wonder how Lay Lay was doing. Despite the way they ended, Ava loved her mother with every fiber of her being. Regardless of how things had left off, Lay Lay was still her mom at the end of the day. She wanted to stop at home for a second, so imagine her surprise when Nique pulled into the driveway of the house. Ava looked at everyone in the car with a confused look on her face, not knowing what was going on.

"Why are we here?"

"This is just the address we were told to come to," Vince said from beside her. They were both in the front row of the van, and he was preparing to get out. "Look, y'all, they said we only have two hours to get this place cleaned. Blane, did you remember your mask? I don't have time for you to be throwing up again, my nigga. You know dead bodies stink."

Dead bodies? Ava's eyes widened, and she looked around at all of them in the car.

"Vince," she breathed as her heartbeat pounded in her ears, "you said that you are cleaners. Exactly what . . . what do you clean?"

Although the question was directed to Vince, Vy was the one who answered. She turned around and looked Ava square in the eyes, not realizing the impact her next words would have on Ava for the rest of her life.

"Murder scenes."

Ava's hand flew to the handle of the door and flung it open. Vince tried to grab her arm before she jumped out of the car, but she snatched away. She ran up the concrete stairs and was at the door in seconds. Instantly, she noticed that the door was slightly cracked, and an unpleasant odor hit her nose before she even pushed the door all the way open.

When she stepped in and flicked the light on, she was at a complete loss for words. The house looked exactly like it did when she left, except the kitchen. What she saw there caused her to let out a bloodcurdling scream. There, bound to a chair with no eyes in his sockets, was Dumphy. His entire body was covered in blood, and so was the tile floor around him. His entire body had deep gashes, and he was missing all of his fingers and toes. Whoever had killed him took their time so that he would feel all of the pain that he possibly could.

Ava was frozen in her tracks and inhaling the funk from his already decaying body until she noticed the bloody handprints on the wall. They were smeared, almost as if someone was being forcefully removed and tried to hold on to the wall.

"Mom!" Ava screamed, running around the house on a mad search. "Mommy!"

She didn't know that she was crying until her chest began heaving. She was so fearful that she would find her mother in the same shape that Dumphy was in. However, when she didn't find her at all, her mind still wasn't eased. Londa and Vy came up behind her in the hallway of the home and tried to get her to calm down, but she swung wild fists, giving them no choice but to back up.

"Stay the fuck away from me!" she screamed and then dropped to her knees, banging her hands on the floor as she heaved. "No, no, no, no, no!"

While Londa and Vy tried to calm her down so that they could all start their job to get paid, Nique had gone into the living room of the house. She thought that Ava was just having a breakdown from seeing the dead body, but when she saw the family portraits on the walls of the house, she knew differently.

"Damn," she said to herself, waving Blane and Vince over to where she was standing by the couch. "Look."

The boys' eyes followed her pointed finger to the pictures above the fireplace. There they saw many photos of Ava with a woman who looked very much like her. The pictures ranged from when Ava was a young girl until now. Suddenly they realized why she was having a breakdown, and they called Vy over to them.

"Yo, Vy," Nique said, glancing over Vy's shoulder to where Ava was kneeling. Her head was buried in Londa's shoulder, and the two were rocking side to side. "This is her people's house."

Vy too stared at the pictures, and she felt chills come over her body. She felt so guilty, although she knew that none of what had taken place was her fault. Still, nobody should have to see their mother's home bloodied up like that.

"Is there another body?"

"Just him," Vince answered, shaking his head. "But those bloody hand marks on the wall look like they belong to a woman. By the way they're skidded all the way down the stairs, they took her with them. That's a lot of blood, though. If it was her mom's, ain't no way she's still alive."

Realizing they'd already lost a valuable fifteen minutes, Vy nodded her head and put the mask that was around her neck over her face. "Londa, take her to the van and sit with her until we're done in here. You will still get your share for the night. Let's just get this place cleaned up and get out of here."

She watched Londa help a limp Ava out of the home, and she couldn't help but wonder what in the world would make her mother a target of King Dex's. Whatever it was, it was bad.

Chapter 6

Knock! Knock!

Glizzy lay in his California king on his back with his right arm over his eyes. He was so engrossed in his own thoughts that he didn't even hear the knock on the door. A few days had passed since his night with the young woman he knew as Cinderella, but he could not get her out of his head. He was sure that if he tried hard enough, he could forget her the way he did any of the women who basically threw themselves at his feet, but he didn't want to try. He still remembered the sweet smell of her skin and the fact that, although her lipstick had faded from drinking out of the club's plastic cups, her lips were still luscious. She was soft-spoken, but he heard every word she said. He didn't know if she was different from the others he'd come across; for all he knew she could have been the exact same. Yet, the possibility that she could be the one to blow his mind was weighing heavy on his shoulders.

He wanted with every fiber of his being to knock off the heads of the men who pulled him away from her that night. However, he knew that his father's henchmen were just doing their job. If anything had happened to Glizzy, King Dex would have rained terror on the whole city. Instead, Glizzy tried every way that he could think of to find out who she was. It was no use. No one at the club that night knew who she was, nor could he locate her on social media. It would have helped if he'd gotten her real name and, had he known the night would end so chaotically, he would have pressed her for it.

Knock! Knock!

That time he couldn't ignore the loud banging on his door. He groaned but got to his feet to see who was so hell-bent on interrupting his thoughts. When he flung open the door, he prepared to greet whoever it was with nasty words, but when he saw the stern face, he quickly pursed his lips.

"I'm going to act like I didn't have to knock on this door twice for you to open it," Whitney, the family housekeeper, said. She was dressed casually in a pair of jeans and a red Nebraska T-shirt, holding an empty basket on her hip. "It's almost noon, boy. I know you weren't in here sleeping. Since you were able to rip and run down these halls, I've never known you to sleep past nine o'clock."

"Well, maybe a lot has changed since I've been gone," Glizzy countered, but Whitney gave him a knowing look.

"A few things have changed, but not that much. Now, move." She pushed him gently out of the way so that she could enter the room. "You didn't bring your clothes to the washroom like I asked you."

"Whitney." Glizzy sighed and plopped back down on his bed. "How many times do I have to tell you that I can wash my own clothes?"

Whitney paid him no mind as she bustled around his room, picking up any stray garment that was out of place. He'd been home for less than a year after being gone for five, but she didn't know why he thought anything would be different when he came back. She couldn't understand how his mother, Shar, could make him clean up after himself. He was the prince, after all. And if Shar didn't want to do it, she could at least hire somebody to do so.

It was no secret that Whitney was not fond of Glizzy's mother. Whitney told King Dex when he first brought her home that she was trouble, but he didn't want to listen. The next thing she knew, Shar and King Dex had given birth to a beautiful baby boy. Now, King Dex may have been a lot of things, but a deadbeat wasn't one of them, which was why when Shar decided to check out of being a mother for a while, King Dex took Glizzy completely under his wing. Now, Whitney was completely opposed to the thought of her precious Glizzy living the street life, but it was inevitable. Not only was he the spitting image of his father, he acted just like him, too. Coming up, he always said he would be the boss just like his daddy. She just wished he could be the boss of something else.

Although King Dex told Whitney that Glizzy left to spend time with his mother, she saw right through that lie. After working with him for so long, she, unknown to him, was privy to all of his plans. At the time of Glizzy's departure, King Dex had been working on expanding to Houston, Texas. Although that was where Shar resided, Whitney already knew the game. Glizzy, always geared up and ready to prove himself to his father, jumped at the chance to be the man in charge of an expansion project.

"I'm grown, Whit." Glizzy grinned at the fuss the older woman was making. "My mama technically didn't have to wash my clothes."

"Hmm." Whitney rolled her eyes. "Well, she could have. Hell, she needed to make up for lost time. When you first went down there, I sent her a list of the things you were accustomed to. You are a prince. There is no reason why you should have been living like a peasant!"

Glizzy burst out laughing, remembering his mother's face when she read the letter from Whitney. Shar was mad for a whole week over it. "Does this heffa forget that I'm the one who pushed you out of my pussy?" she'd said.

In Whitney's defense, she was the one who had practically raised him when Shar and King Dex separated. In the beginning, Glizzy was skeptical about moving to a state he had never been to, but King Dex made sure he was surrounded by familiar faces. At first, Glizzy stayed with Shar, but after six months, he knew he had to branch out on his own. The plan was for him to remain as low-key as possible until every deal was sealed, but when Shar started clocking his pockets and demanding that he pay all of her bills, he knew he had to go. He figured that if he was going to be paying any bills, they would be his own.

Whitney didn't know all of that, though, and he wouldn't tell her. She already hated his mother; it was no secret. Also, things in Houston ended up working out better than he had ever imagined. If it weren't for the fact that his father had requested that he come back to Omaha, he probably would still be out there.

Glizzy opened his mouth to say something else but thought better of it. Although Whitney was technically an employee of his dad's, she was practically like family. He should have been used to people waiting on him hand and foot by then because, like she said, he was a hood prince. He watched her tidy his room all the way up until she got to his closet.

"Wait!" he said, trying to stop her from opening the door, but it was too late.

"Boy!" she exclaimed, setting the basket in her arms on the ground. Kneeling, she grabbed a red boot from the floor of the walk-in closet and turned around to face him. "You cross-dressing now?"

The look of alarm on her face confused Glizzy's insides. He didn't know whether to laugh or be offended that she would even assume such a thing. There was only one way to get out of that one, or else he wouldn't hear the end of it: tell the truth.

"I met a girl the other night."

"You must have done some mighty good sneaking around then," Whitney said, shutting the closet door. "Because I know whenever someone comes in and out of this here house."

"She wasn't here. I met her at the club."

"Oh, you mean the one you almost lost your life at because you want to be fast!"

"Come on now, Whit."

"Don't 'come on now' me, boy. I don't know what it is with you and your father and your infatuation with the fast life."

"How was I supposed to know that they would be shooting?"

"In the path that you're walking, that's something you should expect at all times. Your father told me about how you were upset with his people for getting you out of there."

"Yeah, because they dragged me away from her."

"Her?"

"The girl I met that night." Glizzy sighed in exasperation. "As soon as they started busting, Dad's goons got me out of there. When things cleared up, I ran back in to see if she was okay, but all I found was this shoe."

"And how do you know this is her shoe?"

"Those are special edition Christian Louboutin boots, the same ones that I was going to buy Nisa before she snaked me. I noticed them on Cinderella when I first saw her, and when I found it in the club, I knew it was hers. If she is still alive, she probably hates me."

"Wait." Whitney had to sit down next to him to make sense of what she was being told. "So, her name is Cinderella?"

"Yeah. I mean, no. I never got her full name before all that mess happened."

Whitney pursed her lips and studied the boy she had grown to love like her very own son. She knew when he wasn't acting like himself, and that was one of those times. She had never seen him so out of whack behind a girl. Her hand was on his comforter, and she could feel the warmth from his body. She knew he must have been holed up in that room for a while just lying in bed. He had always been what most would call the "player" type, but she would defend him by saying he was just testing the waters. He was young, so he had every right to date until he found that special girl. His last prospect, Nisa, was one Whitney didn't have to worry about getting too far with her prince. From what he would tell her about Nisa, she already could tell the little heffa was after him for his money and not his heart. Glizzy found that out when he found her in bed with another man.

Whitney cleared her throat and tried to put her words in order. Although she wanted to call him silly, she could tell that this Cinderella girl was weighing heavy on his mind. "So, you really like this girl, huh?"

"Yeah. I mean, I think so," he said, shrugging his shoulders. "I know you're probably thinking I sound silly as hell, but there was something about her, Whit. I just have this feeling that if I would have finished my night off with her, she would have been around for a while. I have this big-ass cloud of 'what if' over my head, and it's eating me alive."

"So, what are you going to do about it?"

"I don't know. What do you think I should do?"

"I think you should finish it the way it started," she said, standing to her feet and picking up her basket. "I think you should throw the biggest party of the year and let the city know you're looking for your Cinderella. If what you're feeling is real, then I can bet my bottom dollar that she is feeling the same emotions."

Glizzy's face broke into a smile, something it hadn't done until she had entered the room. One thing about Whitney was that she always had an answer for everything, and right then her answer was brilliant. "See, this is why I fuck with you, Whit."

"Watch your mouth when you're talking to me, boy," Whitney said, walking toward the door. Right before she closed it, she turned her head to face him. "But you know I fuck with you too, Glizzy. Now, get your handsome self up and come downstairs to get some food!"

Chapter 7

The sound of the metal from the mailbox being lifted got Vy's attention as she was walking by the front door. She was in the kitchen at the time, and all was silent in her home, surprisingly. Her brow raised simply because the mailman had already come that day, and she instantly set all that was in her hands down on the island in her kitchen. Drawing the pistol from her waist, she eased her way to the door and looked through the peephole. When she didn't see anybody but her elderly neighbor, Mr. Vincent, outside doing some lawn work, she opened the door. Stepping out on the porch, she stood there for a second before making another move. Her head turned left and right, eyeing the street and trying to find anything out of place. Whoever had just been at her mailbox was long gone and, from the looks of it, they left something behind.

Pulling the white envelope out of her mailbox, she wasted no time in ripping it open. Inside was a note attached to an invitation with gold lettering. She read the note:

Your services have been requested for the event attached. Please make yourself available an hour before the event and two hours after.

She rolled her eyes, already knowing what that meant. King Dex not only hired them for his dirty laundry, but he also hired them for legit cleaning jobs. It was a way to clean the money that he paid them since, after all, they were his employees. Her eyes switched to the invitation, and she read it out loud. "'Glizzy has formally invited you to the masquerade ball of the year! Please come dressed to flatter and ready to have a good time. P.S. Cinderella, Glizzy is looking for you.' Oh, shit!"

Suddenly, Vy wasn't concerned that whoever had dropped the letter off knew her address. Glizzy, after all, was the son of the man whose payroll she was on. The invitation had a plus one, and Vy knew exactly who she was going to invite. Going back into the house, she picked up everything that she had set down and began again what she had started to do in the first place.

Vy had been nothing but hospitable since Ava had been staying in her large guest room in the basement. She forced Ava to eat and to at least leave her room if she didn't want to leave the house. She felt for Ava, but she was also a realist about situations. Like that morning: she was starting to grow attached to Ava, but she didn't have one friend without a job. She didn't mind Ava staying with her for as long as she needed to, and she didn't expect her to pay any bills. Still, that didn't mean she didn't want her to get on her feet and get some money. She would be a horrible friend if she let Ava mope around and be broke at the same time. Vy didn't care what anybody said; happiness cost money. The only people who were happy broke were the homeless, and even they posted on every corner and begged for change. The way she saw it, the more Ava didn't move around, the deeper the depression she was in would get. She needed to keep herself busy so her thoughts would eventually transform themselves.

She sauntered down the stairs in her home, fully dressed in a long-sleeved shirt and a pair of her favorite skinny jeans. As soon as her feet touched the soft carpet in her basement, she headed toward the guest bedroom where Ava had been staying the past three days. In her arms, she carried a tray of food along with some orange juice and two shots of tequila. She knocked on the door to let Ava know she was there before twisting the knob.

"I come bearing gifts," she said with a smile as she entered the room. "Bacon, eggs, and toast. Nothing too heavy for you."

She was pleased to see that Ava was sitting at the burgundy vanity and that the room was brightly lit. Ava was fully dressed in jeans with the knees cut out and a black off-the-shoulder tunic sweater. Her hair had been neatly placed into two braids, and she was putting the finishing touches on her eyebrows when Vy set the tray on the bed.

"Thank you," Ava said, giving Vy a small smile back. "It smells good."

"It tastes good, too. I know because I stole a piece of your bacon on the way down here." Vy grinned. "You look nice. Going somewhere?"

"No." Ava shrugged her shoulders, standing up and heading over to her food. "I'm just tired of looking crazy. Thank you for letting me stay here. I know I haven't been that good of a house guest since . . ."

She let her voice trail off, but Vy knew what she was trying to say. She watched the pain that Ava was wearing on the inside fight hard to show on her face. Vy felt for her deeply and, as a person who'd lost both of her parents, she knew that the pain Ava was feeling would never go away. She sighed and sat down on the bed beside Ava, grabbing both shots from the tray.

"Here," she said, handing Ava hers. "Let's take these first, and then I'm going to put you up on game."

Ava hesitated to take the alcohol, but then suddenly she yearned to feel the burning sensation trickle down her throat. When she grabbed the large shot, she and Vy clinked glasses before downing the liquid. The orange juice was supposed to be the chaser, but neither reached for it. Vy sat there with her eyes closed and let the alcohol lift the buzz she already had.

"I've already been drinking this morning," Vy said, opening her eyes, "so please excuse me if this comes out a little harsh. Look, I know it's only been three days, and the shit that you're feeling is unbearable."

"What would you know about my pain? You don't know what I'm feeling. You don't have any worries in the world."

"Oh, but I do," Vy said, shooting sharp eyes in Ava's direction. "You're looking at the shit I have now and assuming that I have never struggled. Both of my parents were murdered when I was sixteen. Sixteen! Imagine being a pretty sixteen-year-old with a blossomed body in the system. I lost my virginity to the man who was supposed to be my foster father two weeks after being placed in the home that he shared with his wife. I tried to tell my caseworker, but she just placed me in another home. That time my foster parents' son had his way with me. The shit kept happening until I ran away when I was seventeen. I didn't have any money, didn't even graduate high school. But by the grace of God, I ran into somebody who was able to put me on this cleaning business. It may be a little unconventional, but hey, shit happens. People get killed every day, and I am paid well to clean it up. So, see, I didn't have time to mourn their deaths, because I was too busy trying to survive.

"You're hurt, Ava. You have every right to feel that hurt, but don't let it become you. The past is something that is not changeable. You just have to figure out where to position your future. This house, my cars? That is how I repositioned my pain. By doing for myself what keeps me happy. You are the only one in control of your emotions, so feel that pain, but check that shit at the door. We gotta put you on to some money, mama. You've been stuck in this house for too long."

At first, Ava wanted to be argumentative, but the more Vy spoke, the more she had to admit that she made sense. There was nothing that she could do to change the past. The only thing she could fix was the future. She clenched her eyes shut and inhaled deeply right before the tears slid from her eyes.

"This pain," she whispered, shaking her head. "This pain in my chest is never going to go away. Not until I find out what happened to her."

Vy reached and grabbed Ava's hand and squeezed it. It was quivering ever so slightly. "I need to tell you something, Ava," she said when the final tears had fallen from Ava's eyes. "About what may have happened to your mother."

Ava's eyes met Vy's serious expression, and her brow furrowed. If she knew something about her mother's death, why would she just now be saying something?

"You weren't in the state of mind to hear what I'm about to tell you." Vy answered Ava's silent question. "And, honestly, I still don't think you are, but then again you might never be ready, so I'm just going to tell you. With this cleaning job, our team works for one person: King Dex."

"Okay."

"That means any job we get sent on to do, it's his dirty work."

Her words suddenly clicked in Ava's head, and her throat contracted. It was as if someone were choking her and cutting off all of her access to the air around her. If she weren't already sitting down, she would have fallen on the king-sized bed.

"What?" she managed to stammer.

"I'm saying that if we were called to your home to do a cleaning job, then King Dex was behind the murder. So, if you want to know what happened to her, he's who you would have to ask."

Ava knew that would be like asking to die herself, but still, she wanted to know what happened to her mom, or at least where her body was, to give her a proper burial. Rage filled her, and her hands balled into tight fists. She didn't just want to ask him a question; she wanted him dead.

"How do I get close to him? Close enough to hurt him?"

Vy laughed slightly before seeing Ava's stony expression. "Oh, shit. You're serious?"

When Ava nodded her head, letting Vy know just how serious she was, Vy pulled the invitation out from under the tray of food. Ava took it and read it to herself, suddenly feeling a jolt of butterflies.

"Looks like your lover boy is looking for you," Vy said as Ava read and reread the words after the "P.S."

"What does this have to do with anything?"

"It has everything to do with it. Glizzy is King Dex's son." Vy made the revelation, and Ava's eyes widened.

"His . . . son?"

Vy heard the disappointment in Ava's voice and gave her a sad smile. "Yeah, I'm sorry, boo. But if you want to do to King Dex what you're implying, you best stay away from Glizzy. You may be the Cinderella he's looking for, but he rides hard for his daddy."

"I understand." Ava swallowed hard. With her fingers, she traced the lettering, and almost smiled to herself at the subliminal message in the words.

"Who could blame him? You were looking bad as hell the night y'all met." Vy nudged her playfully but then got back to business. "King Dex has requested that my team be cleaners at this event. These jobs are usually two bands each, up front. I'm going to make a phone call and plug you so that no one is surprised to see your face when we pull up. The invite said the party isn't until the end of the month, so we have a few weeks to train your ass how to shoot a gun."

"Vy?" Ava asked, but Vy kept talking like she hadn't heard her.

"We need a plan. King Dex isn't just any nigga. You aren't going to be able to just run up on him. Shit, you won't even be able to take two steps toward him without being used as target practice. I need to talk to Blane."

"Vy!" Ava yelled, and Vy finally stopped talking and looked at her like she was crazy. "I'm sorry, but why are you helping me? Isn't he your boss? If something happens to him, you'll be out of a job."

Vy didn't answer for a minute. She stood up and made like she was about to leave the room so that Ava could eat her breakfast. When she was almost completely out the door, she looked back to Ava and then shrugged her shoulders with a faint smile. When she spoke, her voice was low, but Ava heard every word.

"I don't know how to explain it, but I'm a firm believer in signs, especially when it comes to the people I choose to have in my circle. It wasn't a coincidence that we met at the restaurant. You were supposed to come out to the club with us that night because you were supposed to ride with us on that cleaning job. On top of that, you didn't call the cops when you saw all that you saw. You're solid. Something is telling me that you are supposed to be in my life and that I'm supposed to be in yours. Not on any creepy lesbian shit, either. But everybody needs somebody, and right now we don't have anybody but each other and the team. We're a family full of misfits. Time doesn't warrant a tight bond. The others fuck with you tough too already. You just fit. Like I said, we don't have anybody but each other. Plus, if the situation were turned and you were in my shoes, you would do the same thing."

Ava thought about how they didn't leave her in the club when the shooting started. They'd come back for her. She thought about how kind Vy had been to her. She had felt alone for so long, and finally she felt like she fit somewhere. The death of her mom had done something to her spirit, but all the love surrounding her did something to her heart.

"Thank you," was all Ava could muster without crying.

"Don't thank me, and don't worry about the job. Everybody underground knows my team are the best cleaners in the game. It won't be hard for us to find a new employer. Shit, I heard in Detroit they're paying almost ten bands a job. But eat your food. I'm about to call Blane and Vince crazy asses over here so we can make some moves."

With that, she left Ava alone to eat her food. It had gotten cold while she and Vy were having their heart-to-heart, but it was still good. She waited another hour to leave her room and go up the stairs, and when she finally made her way, she was welcomed by Blane and Vince. They were sitting at the island with Vy, seemingly in a deep discussion.

"What's popping, superstar?" Blane said, being that he was the first one to spot her.

Vince whipped around on his barstool and raised his eyebrow at her. "Damn, girl! You're quiet like a ninja." He turned to Vy and nodded his head. "Aw yeah, I like her. That's a good trait to have."

"Come sit down, Ava," Vy told her, standing up and offering her seat. "We were just talking a little bit about your dilemma, and I think we have a solution."

"Hey, y'all." Ava greeted the guys but didn't take Vy's seat. She went and stood next to her instead. "She told y'all about what I want to do?"

"Yeah. And, first of all, I just want to say I'm sorry about your loss. For real, baby girl. Losing a parent ain't for nothing, man, but we got you," Blane said, but before Ava could thank him, he cut her off. "Second of all, I just want to know if you're out of your damn mind. You've been down in that basement getting high off some shit, huh? What was it, reefer? Crack? Heroin? Because it had to have been some strong shit if you're trying to make a hit at King Dex!"

"Blane!" Vy said and punched him in the arm.

"Okay, my bad," Blane said, rubbing his arm, and a grin spread across his face. Leaning down, he grabbed a black backpack that was on the ground by his feet. "I just had to get that out, but I'm back. Before we leave for some target practice today, I think we need to change something. I think that gun we gave you the other night was too much for you right now. Let's see what you can do with this Ruger."

He pulled the black gun from his bag, and that time Ava didn't hesitate to grab it. It was lighter in her hand than the Glock, and instantly she was drawn to it.

"Ay! Ay!" Vince jumped off of the barstool he was sitting on. He fell on his side to the ground with his hands up when Ava aimed the weapon in his direction. "Girl, what is wrong with you? You the only one in this room who can't shoot a gun and you gon' point that motherfucka at me!"

For the first time in what felt like a long time, Ava laughed. Soon they were all cracking up, simply because Vince looked so ridiculous.

"I'm sorry for laughing, bro, but you just looked like a straight punk!"

"You wouldn't be saying that if she was pointing at you," Vince said, getting back to his feet. "But back to business. Ava, I know you want to get back at King Dex for what he did to your moms and all, but we have to be smart about it, or else all of our heads will be on sticks, and I like my head the way it is, feel me?"

"Tell her what's up," Vy spoke in an eager voice.

"Damn, nigga, can I get there?" Vince turned his attention back to Ava. "Look, word in the business is that King Dex is looking for a cleaner for his house. I've seen what he does in other people's homes. I can only imagine what kinds of shit he does to his enemies in his own."

"You think he takes niggas to his house?" Blane asked in a challenging tone.

"Hell yeah! Especially if them niggas ain't never gon' make it back out."

"You have a point."

"I know I said I would plug you with the job at the event," Vy jumped in, "but this will put you even closer to King Dex. I'd rather plug you for that instead. What do you think?"

"I don't . . . I don't know. I thought that y'all would be with me and—"

"Glizzy lives there," Vy said in a taunting voice.

"I'll do it."

Chapter 8

"You must be Ava!" a welcoming voice rang out.

Ava was standing outside the biggest house she'd ever seen in her life, and it was so elegant that she would never have thought something like it would be in Nebraska. The land surrounding was completely free, and the closest house was half a mile down the road. If she could take a guess, there were probably at least eight bedrooms inside of it and at least two kitchens. She couldn't wait to see if she was right.

It was the first day of her new job, and she was dressed in a simple white sweatshirt that accented her curves and a pair of jeans that made her butt look a little plumper. It was a little chilly outside, but the weather had started to warm up to where you didn't need a coat if you didn't want to wear one. Ava must have been standing there looking lost because the older woman in front of her took a step back and raised her eyebrow at her.

"You are Ava, right? From the Maid for You service?"

"Oh!" Ava finally snapped out of it. "Yes, that's me. Ava Dunning. I'm sorry. I was just mesmerized by this house. Oh, my God, it's gorgeous."

"Thank you!" The smile returned to the woman's face, and she moved out of the way so that Ava could enter. "Well, Miss Ava, I'm Whitney. I'll be showing you around and how to do your job."

Ava felt a rush of cold air hit her skin the moment she walked across the threshold. The sound of running water caught her off guard. She turned her head in the direction it was coming from.

"Is that a fountain?" Ava asked, walking toward it. She touched the water.

Whitney found herself smiling at the girl's amazement at something that had become normal to her. "Yes, honey. That big pond-looking thing with the angel spewing water from its mouth is a fountain."

Ava felt her cheeks grow hot from embarrassment. She hated the fact that she'd just made herself seem like she wasn't used to seeing nice things. Whitney touched her arm gently with her hand and then let it go.

"Don't be embarrassed, honey. I'm just giving you a hard time. Sometimes I think I've been away from the hood for too long. I'm starting to act bourgeoisie like these white folks!" Whitney looked around Ava as if she was looking for something more than the young girl. "Where are your bags, baby?"

"Bags?"

"Yes, bags. Did you think King Dex was going to make you drive to and from work every day? He may be a lot of things, but inconsiderate he is not. I'll just have Glizzy take you to grab some things later."

"Glizzy?" Ava felt her face get hot and looked away to evade Whitney's curious stare.

Ava didn't see Whitney's small smirk because it left as quickly as it came. She held her arm out for Ava to latch on to, which she did, and she led her away from the front door. It was time to show her to the room that she would be staying in. She took Ava on a small tour of the home, showing her all that she could on the way to where they were going. It turned out that the home did have two kitchens like Ava guessed; however, there were only six bedrooms. They passed a few other housekeepers, and what Ava noticed about them was that they were all much older than she.

"Your room is going to be on the second floor," Whitney told her when they got to a stairwell in the back of the house. "I made sure that your room was prepped and ready to stay in yesterday, so you should find it to your liking."

"And don't mind the rats. They're just not used to any-one being in that room," a deep voice said out of nowhere.

Both women turned to see where the voice had come from, and Ava felt her heart drop into her stomach. She thought that she'd be given enough time to get her wits together before she saw Glizzy, but there she was staring into his face and feeling weak in her knees. He wore a white Levi's T-shirt with red lettering and a pair of light denim jeans. It was apparent that he had been just lounging in the house, because on his feet he wore a pair of slide-on house shoes. He was seated at the large kitchen table and had a lot of paperwork in front of him.

Although Ava wasn't intoxicated that time, she felt the exact same way that she did when she first laid eyes on him. Instantly, her hand went to her hair, making sure there were no pieces sticking out. She tried to make the gesture look as casual as she could, but Glizzy's smile in her direction let her know that it didn't look as subtle as she'd hoped.

"Glizzy, boy! What have I told you about sneaking around this house?"

"Technically, y'all snuck up on me. I was sitting at this table this whole time," he said and then turned his attention back to Ava. "Who is this?"

"This is the new maid your father hired to help me around here. Ava, this is Glizzy."

"Nice to meet you," Ava said, and at the sound of her voice, Glizzy's eyebrow shot up.

"Do I know you from somewhere?" he asked skeptically, almost hopeful. There was something very familiar about her eyes, but he couldn't place where he knew her from. "You just seem so familiar to me."

"No," Ava stammered out quickly and cleared her throat. "I think I would remember meeting such a hand-some face."

The two of them stared at each other for a few seconds more, and Ava hoped that he didn't press the issue. She wanted to tell him that she was the girl he'd been looking for, but she also knew that wasn't what she was there for.

Keep your eyes on the prize, Ava, she told herself.

"So, you were about to show me to my room?" She turned back to Whitney, who was giving both of them a curious look.

Whitney wasn't able to get a word out because at that same exact moment, one of the other housekeepers ran into the kitchen seemingly out of breath. She was an older black woman who was probably the same age as Whitney, but Whitney was Angela Bassett fine. The new woman was just petite and cute for her age.

"What is it, Karen?" Whitney asked, placing a hand on Karen's shoulder. "You look like you just saw a ghost."

"Girl! Now, don't you be mad at me when I tell you this. I told the heffa to leave shit alone!"

"Just spit it out!"

"Alayna done spilled the beans all on the floor in the main kitchen!"

"The beans?" Whitney hollered with so much alarm in her voice that you would have thought someone had just died. "I told that woman to leave my baked beans alone. I'm going to kick that woman's ass! Glizzy, would you please show Ava to her room? I'm sorry, honey. I'll be upstairs to get you once I'm done."

"It's okay," Ava tried to say, but Whitney and Karen had already taken off.

Ava felt like a red spot on the wall standing there in front of Glizzy like that. She could feel his eyes on her, so she looked at everything but him, which in turn made it obvious that she was avoiding his gaze.

"I make you nervous or something?"

Why is his voice so damn sexy?

"No," she said out loud, finally making eye contact. "What makes you say that?"

"It's just an effect I seem to have on the ladies." Glizzy shrugged his shoulders nonchalantly.

"That's assuming that I find you attractive." Ava mimicked his shrug. "And, I mean, you *a'ight,* I guess."

"Funny gal, I see." Her wittiness put a grin on Glizzy's face, and he waved her over to the table. "Come look at these designs and tell me which ones you like. I'm having a masquerade ball soon, and I don't know which one I like better."

She did as he asked and went to look at the designs he had spread out all over the table. She had to admit, she was impressed. There was a pamphlet of the ballroom that the party would be at, and it looked huge. Of course, she didn't know why she would expect anything but the best from the kingpin's son. She stared at the designs for a good five minutes before pointing at a champagne-and-gold theme.

"I like this one," she said. "No matter what kind of event you're having, these colors will coincide with everything. The silverware, however, should match those crystal chandeliers, and instead of a rock décor, there should be rose petals on every table."

Glizzy picked up the paper with the color scheme she liked best and leaned back in his seat. He closed his eyes and easily visualized everything that Ava was saying, and he smiled. He liked it. He liked it a lot.

"If only you knew how easy you just made my job. Thank you."

"Women have a better eye for things like that," Ava responded, stepping back from the table. "Now, could you please show me my room? I kind of want to sit down before I start doing real work."

"My bad." Glizzy hopped up. "I almost forgot that you weren't here to just keep me company, ma. Let's go."

She followed him up the flight of stairs and onto the next level of the house. At the end of the wide hallway, it opened up to a circle with three doors. Straight ahead was a large bathroom, and directly across from each other were two bedrooms.

"I never understood why there is a bathroom right there," Glizzy said and stopped in front of one of the bedroom doors. "Both of these rooms have bathrooms in them. Whoever designed this house just was doing shit."

When he opened the door to the bedroom and flicked on the switch, Ava couldn't stop herself from grabbing hold of his arm. Her mouth dropped open, and her eyes couldn't believe how lavish the room was. The king-sized bed sat in the center of the room and had a white see-through canopy. She'd always wanted one of those. To the right in the corner was a vanity two times the size of the one she had at Vy's house, and the dressers along the left wall were so elegant they looked like something straight out of a Disney movie. The carpet looked like it was brand new, and the closet was behind the bed, to the back of the room. It had double doors, and Ava could already tell just by looking that it was huge.

"I thought," Ava whispered, still clenching Glizzy's arm, "you said that there was a bathroom in here?"

"It's in the closet," he said, grinning down at her. "Are you going to give me my arm back?"

"Oh!" Ava let him go instantly. "I'm sorry. It's just that . . . Wow. This is where I'll be staying? I thought I would just have a regular old room."

"Nah." Glizzy shook his head. "My dad wouldn't do you like that. He treats everyone who enters his home like family."

Sauntering into the room, Ava began making her way around it. That was the second time in one day that she heard something nice about King Dex, but she knew better than to believe it. "Your father sounds like a good man."

Glizzy watched her and put his hands in his pockets. She was beautiful, there was no doubt about that. His eyes traveled from her hair all the way to her hips as they switched when she walked. Ever since that night at the club, he hadn't been able to even look at a woman the same because he was so focused on finding his Cinderella. However, there he was seemingly intrigued by a woman who had barely said four sentences to him.

"That just depends on who's saying it," he answered with a shrug. "To some he has been a blessing, but to others he has been a monster. But, with most humans, in order to see that monster come out, you have to do something. I would give you an example, but you're a cleaner, so I'm sure you've seen some of his handiwork."

"How do you know that I am a cleaner?"

"I make it my business to know a little something about everyone around me. I knew that King Dex was hiring an in-house cleaner. I just didn't know that you would be so beautiful."

"You have such a way with the ladies, don't you?"

"I do, but that was both a compliment and a question. How did a woman as beautiful as you end up in a profession so dirty?"

"The money is good," Ava said simply, batting her long lashes slightly. "Plus, I've never been afraid to get my hands a little dirty. We live in a world where shit goes bump in the night quite often, and somebody needs to be there to clean up the mess."

She felt like she sounded believable only because, prior to her starting the job, she'd gone on a few other cleaning jobs with her crew. In a matter of weeks, she'd gone from a waitress at a restaurant to a woman who knew how to dispose of dead bodies. Working with Vy and the others made her feel as if she'd been working as a cleaner for years, and being used to the sight of blood was becoming second nature to her.

Glizzy stared at her for a few more moments before he reached for the door handle to shut it and give her some privacy. "It was nice to meet you, Ava."

"You too, Glizzy," Ava told him. Before he could shut the door all the way, she called out to him. "Wait! I didn't know that I would be staying here, so I didn't bring any clothes. Whitney said that you might be able to take me by a few stores later?"

"Yeah, that's cool. Let me go handle some business and we can go in a few hours."

"Thank you."

"No problem," he said and glanced at her one last time. "Are you sure I don't know you from somewhere?"

"Maybe." Ava caught herself before she said too much. "Maybe from another lifetime. You know they say energies always recognize each other, even in other lives."

Glizzy eyed her for a few more moments, and for a second, she felt like he didn't believe a word she had said. Finally, a small smirk came across his face.

"Okay, Erykah Badu. Be ready when I come back."

With that, he was gone.

Being in Glizzy's all-black Jeep Wrangler alone with him made Ava nervous. He told her he was taking her to the Oakview mall, and the whole ride she took notice of him stealing glances at her.

"I can see you staring at me, you know."

"My bad, it's just . . . Never mind. You know where you want to shop? I don't think Forever 21 is in this mall."

"Forever 21?"

"Yeah." He looked at her. "You too good for normal stores? Or is my dad paying that well these days?"

"Nah, I shop there. You just don't look like you would step foot in a store like that."

"Why? Because I'm rich?"

"No. I mean, yeah."

"Ma, to me clothes are clothes. I have expensive tastes with a few pieces, like Ralph Lauren." He jokingly rubbed his hand from his chest to his stomach, showcasing the jacket of the Ralph Lauren sweat suit he was wearing. "But that's just some nigga shit. Niggas love Polo, and I fit the bill for that. But real shit, if I like it, I buy it. Whether it's five bucks or a thousand."

"I hear you. I'm going to be shopping on a budget today. I'm trying to save for a place."

"Well, then, today is your lucky day. Don't worry about spending anything. It's on me," he said when they pulled up in Dillard's parking lot.

"You don't have to do that, Glizzy."

"I know, but I want to."

He got out of the car first and then came to open her door. He helped her out of the car, and the two of them walked in the mall side by side together. It was as if everybody knew who Glizzy was, the way eyes instantly fell on the two of them. Some people looked at him with adoration and made sure to speak as he passed, while others stared with contempt. She even got a few hateful stares from women when they saw that Ava was with him. It was the oddest thing ever for Ava to experience, and she wondered how Glizzy felt about it.

"Damn, you're a star," she said after a group of kids asked to have a picture with him.

"A prince," he corrected with a wink. "It has its ups and downs."

"I'm surprised you don't have security with you."

"Look behind you."

Ava did as he instructed, and he didn't even have to tell her what to look for. Her eyes instantly lay on two big, burly men, dressed casually, walking behind them. They kept their distance, but they were still in range to hop into action if need be.

"That's you?"

"Yeah," Glizzy answered. "I can handle myself. I fear no nigga. But my pops ain't for none of that. You want to go in here?"

They were outside of Victoria's Secret, and Ava's entire face lit up. It had been so long since she was able to feel the fabric of Vicky's Secret on her body, and she was tired of Hanes. Glizzy saw the happy glint in her eyes and laughed— Not at her, but at how simple she was to please. When they entered, he took three bags from one of the employees and gave them to Ava.

"Get whatever you want," he said and turned back to the brown-skinned employee. From his pocket, he pulled out a crisp hundred-dollar bill and pointed at Ava. "See to it that she doesn't have to search for anyone when she needs help with something."

"No problem, Glizzy." The young girl batted her eyelashes at him and headed toward Ava. "Hi, ma'am, I'm Destiny. Is there anything I can help you find?"

They spent almost an hour in the store alone and left with two big bags filled to the top. Ava tried to carry them, but Glizzy wouldn't let her. By the end of the day, Ava had all of the things that she needed and more than enough stuff that she didn't need.

"You spent like three thousand dollars on me today," Ava said, looking at all of her bags in the back seat. "Did you even get yourself anything?"

"Yeah."

"What?" Ava asked, scanning the bags for something of his.

"The smile on your face."

Ava pursed her lips to hide the grin forcing its way up, and she playfully nudged him. "Shut up." She rolled her eyes and had to turn away because she couldn't stop smiling.

"I'm for real, though," Glizzy told her. "It's refreshing to be with someone who appreciates the little things. These girls out here don't see me as shit but a walking dollar sign. They are never interested in knowing me for me."

"Who are you?"

"I'm just a nigga who wants to enjoy life. Straight up. I wanna love and be loved back."

His answer was so simple but said so many different things to her. She understood exactly what he meant.

"Because, with all that, everything else should fall rightfully in place." She spoke her thoughts out loud.

The smile was gone from her face, but when Glizzy averted his eyes from the road to steal a glance at her, he saw that the smile was still in her eyes. He had just met her, but he felt like he'd known her for a while. That whole day he'd laughed more than he had that entire month. He was allowed to let go and act his age for once. In the life that he lived, there was little to no room for fun, because fun always got interrupted by business. Earlier he told her that today was her lucky day, but in all actuality, it was his. He was able to mix business with a dab of innocent pleasure.

"Exactly," he finally said. "You asked me who I am; now it's my turn to ask, who are you?"

"Me? I'm just a girl still trying to find her way. I don't know what I want, and I like it."

"I get it, no expectations."

"Right," Ava said and then looked at the palms of her hands. "My life has been filled with so many disappointments already. But I recently figured out that I have control of what disappoints me, so I try to position everything accordingly."

"I feel that," Glizzy said.

"So, besides the fact that you feel that women are gold-diggers, why are you single?"

"Because I haven't found the right woman yet," he told her.

"So, nobody has caught your eye?" she pressed a little too eagerly. He was quiet for a second, but then he chuckled to himself. "What?"

"This is going to sound crazy," he started, "but a little while ago, I met this girl. She was the most beautiful woman I've ever seen in my life. She was just different from all these other women. I could tell just by the way she presented herself. But that was the first and last time I saw her."

"Sounds like love at first sight," Ava joked, but his response shocked her.

"Yeah. Maybe."

"She didn't tell you her name?"

They stopped at a red light, and instantly Ava regretted pressing the subject. Glizzy turned to face her, and he stared into her eyes intently. His gaze was so powerful that she almost looked away from him.

"Cinderella. She told me her name was Cinderella."

Ava faked a laugh and a bewildered expression. "Cinderella? She couldn't come up with something more creative?"

Glizzy didn't say anything; he was too busy studying her face, almost like he was looking for a lie. Ava held her breath, certain that she'd been found out, but when the light turned green and his eyes were back on the road, she let it out.

"Right." Glizzy shook his head. "And I hate that all these girls are into wearing wigs and shit. I don't know if I would even recognize her if I were as close to her as I am to you right now."

"You'd know," Ava told him and could have kicked herself again.

"How so?"

"Because, if what you feel is real, it will be reciprocated to you. She won't be able to stay away."

"I'm counting on it. That's why I'm throwing this ball. I hope she comes out, just so I don't have that 'what if' shit over me forever." He changed the subject suddenly. "Passing all these restaurants has me a little hungry. You gon' let me wine and dine you before we head back to the house?"

"You say that like this is a date."

"It can't be?" Glizzy asked with a sneaky smile.

As much as Ava would have loved to sit across from him and allow him to pick her mind, she feared too much would come out of her mouth, especially if wine was involved. She could picture it: *"I'm the girl you met that night, but I'm also only here so that I can kill your father because he killed my mother."* What a disaster that would be. So, she declined his offer as politely as she could.

"I'm not really hungry. You've spent so much money on me already. I don't want you to waste more on a meal. Plus, Whitney seems like the type to throw down in the kitchen. I'm sure I'll grab a bite later on."

"True that," Glizzy said, although she could hear the disappointment in his voice. "No worries. I'm sure I'ma see you around."

"Yeah, since I'm your employee," Ava reminded him.

"You're King Dex's employee."

"Same thing."

The rest of the ride back out to the house was made without them talking. Glizzy turned on some music while Ava's hand itched. She couldn't wait to get back so she could call Vy and tell her about the day's events. Phase one, "Infiltrate the Home," was complete.

Chapter 9

Ava didn't know how it happened. She tried her hardest to keep things strictly professional while she was inside King Dex's home, but no matter what, she couldn't deny her attraction to Glizzy. Since she'd been there, not a day went by that she didn't see or speak to him. She was honestly starting to think that he sought her out, which she didn't mind. She tried to keep her eyes on the prize, but whenever she saw King Dex, even in his house, he had a guard with him. The day that Whitney assigned her to his room, she knew that wouldn't be a good idea.

"I have the pool, the basement, and the wine cellar today, Whit," she tried to reason. "Plus, I thought you enjoyed cleaning your little Glizzy's room."

The two of them were in the main kitchen at the time, sorting through the silverware for the ball that upcoming weekend. There was still a lot of work to be done, but they were making very good time. They were both dressed in jeans and matching long-sleeved T-shirts, with white Nike Roshes on their feet.

"I do," Whitney said and then gave her a knowing glance. "But something tells me that you would too."

Ava turned her head away and began to roll a set of silverware into a gold napkin. "I don't have a clue what you're talking about," she said.

"You don't have a clue, my pretty brown ass," Whitney said, placing her hand on her hip. "I see the way he looks at you, but more importantly I see the way you look at him. I was born at night, but not last night! You two like each other, and if you're going to see him, I'd rather you be working when you do it, not sneaking off and leaving me to peel a hundred potatoes by myself!"

Ava's eyes widened, and she bit her lips. It was no use; the giggle snuck its way through. She knew what day Whitney was speaking of, and by the time Ava showed her face to help, Whitney was already done— and in a sour mood, too.

"I said I was sorry, Whit! Plus, I'm still kind of new. In the real world, I would still be in training right about now."

"Well, this ain't a corporate job now, is it?" Whitney asked and swatted the young girl playfully on her arm. "Now, I want you to go up to th—"

"You two ladies are doing a spectacular job!"

The voice boomed loudly, but not in volume. Ava felt the hairs on the back of her neck stand up and, she swallowed hard, almost scared to look up. She tried to even her breathing and focus on the silverware that she had in her hand, but even her hands had started shaking.

"Dex! Don't be frightening us like that now!" Whitney chastised King Dex like he was her son. "And why do you bring this big, burly man everywhere you go, even in your own house?"

"Because, Whit," King Dex said, leaning in and kissing her on the cheek, "you never know where an enemy is lurking."

"Well, ain't no enemies in this house now. And you know how I feel about y'all having those guns around me."

Ava continued to work on the task at hand as they went back and forth. She felt the temperature in the room change, but she didn't know if it was her fear or his aura. When he finally spoke to her, she almost jumped out of her shoes.

"You must be the new maid we hired," he said and held his hand out for Ava to shake it.

Ava stared at it for a few seconds before placing a meek hand inside of it. When she finally looked into his face, she was taken aback. He was just an older version of his son. It was almost as if he himself had spit Glizzy out. She wondered what she would do in the moment when she faced him face to face. Would she yell? Would she call him a murderer and shoot him right in the throat? She thought that he would look like an evil monster, but there he was standing in front of her, casually wearing a pair of workout shorts and a T-shirt that showed off every muscle on his upper body. He looked . . . normal. Ava forced a smile on her face.

He killed your mother. He has to die.

Out of the corner of her eye, she saw the big chef's knife that Whitney had used to cut an apple a little bit earlier. All Ava had to do was grab it and slit his throat; however, the iron grip that he had on her hand told her that she wouldn't be able to move fast enough.

"How have you liked working for Maid for You?" he asked, calling his cleaning service by its business name.

"It's a job," Ava responded, releasing his hand. "Some of the jobs are dirtier than others, and I feel that we should be compensated more. Especially since we are one of the best cleaning teams."

"You work with Vy, right?"

"Yes."

"Yeah, they are one of my more thorough teams. Roscoe!" King Dex spoke to the big, burly man in the suit standing at the entrance to the kitchen.

"Yes, sir?"

"Make a note to be sure that Vy's cleaning team receives two thousand dollars more a job, no matter how dirty."

"Of course, sir." Roscoe nodded.

"How does that sound?" King Dex turned back to Ava.

"The others will be happy."

"Why are you in such a good mood today, King?" Whitney asked, crossing her arms.

"I'm not," King Dex told her, going in the fridge. "I just got off the phone with Dorian, and it has come to my attention that I am at a loss of fifty thousand dollars."

Whitney shook her head. "I told your ass not to trust those damn crackheads," Whitney said. "I knew Dumphy's mama, and she wasn't shit either! I don't know why you would trust him."

Ava had gone to the sink to rinse off a box of silverware that she had just opened, but at the mention of Dumphy's name, it felt like time around her had frozen.

"I didn't trust him," King Dex said simply. He grabbed a cold bottle of water and shut the refrigerator door. "I put him and his partner in a position to gain my trust. I have always believed in love reciprocation, and with those two I failed. Whereas I might not have gotten my money back, they paid for it in other ways."

"Mmm, I hear you, baby. Since you were young, you always had a good heart. Where is Dorian, and why the hell hasn't he been by the house?"

"He's tying up a loose end for me right now. He'll be here once he's done with that."

"What happened to the woman?"

"That's the loose end. He's dropping her body off right now."

"Excuse me," Ava said, turning back to the table and setting the silverware down. "It was nice to meet you. Whit, I'm heading upstairs if you need me."

She didn't wait for either of them to say anything to her before she made a swift getaway. As she walked, King Dex watched her curiously. There was something about the tone of voice in which she spoke to him that didn't sit right with him. It was forced. Whitney saw his eyes, and she hit his arm.

"Uh-uh. That's all Glizzy. That boy hasn't been able to stay away from her since she got here."

"What's her name again?"

"Ava. Ava Dunning."

King Dex's brow furrowed. "Interesting."

The first thing Ava did as soon as she got upstairs to Glizzy's room was call Vy when she saw that he wasn't in there. She told her all about the exchange between her and King Dex.

"He killed your mother behind a debt that her boyfriend owed him?"

"Yes," Ava answered, sitting on the bed. "Her body is being dropped off tonight. I need to know where."

She finally understood why there was so much blood. She steadied her breathing and tried not to think about how many times she had told her mother to leave Dumphy's no-good ass alone. He was toxic and a waste of a man. Ava didn't know what she wanted to do anymore. Although she was still angry, she now had a better understanding of the situation.

"That's tough," Vy said, and it seemed like there was more she wanted to say, but she didn't.

So, Ava said it for her. "That's the game, huh? I'm going to make him tell me where she's being taken tonight."

"What about the ball?"

"Fuck the ball."

There was silence on the other end of the line for a brief moment.

"Do you have your gun?"

Ava thought about the gun that she tucked in her pants the first day she walked in the home. It was hidden well under the sweatshirt she had on, and she was pleased that nobody checked her at the door.

"Yes. The guards change shifts at midnight. That's when I'm going to do it."

"Okay. I'll be there to get you if . . . if—"

"If I come out alive? I will, I promise."

"Promise what?"

Ava hadn't even heard the room door open behind her. She turned her head and saw Glizzy standing there in nothing but a pair of cotton shorts that sagged ever so slightly, showing off his Ralph Lauren boxers. She was caught off guard not by his presence, but by how sexy he looked standing there staring at her with a confused look on his face.

"I'll call you back," she said into her phone.

"Remember: midnight!"

"Okay," she said and hung up the phone. She stood up and turned to Glizzy. "I'm sorry. Whit told me to come up here and tidy up your room."

"It doesn't look like you were doing that much tidying to me," he told her. "And why you in my room on the phone with niggas?"

Ava looked at him like he was crazy, but the serious look on his face amused her. If she had to take a guess, she would have said that he was feeling a little jealous. "And why do you think I was on the phone with a nigga? Better yet, why would you care?"

"I don't," he said, plopping down on his bed. "And I told Whitney that I'm a grown-ass man and I don't need anybody cleaning up after me."

"You sure?" Ava said and pointed at the dirty clothes basket. "Because that shit looks like it's been there for weeks."

She winked at him and made her way to where the basket was next to the closet door. She scooped it up and opened the closet at the same time to make sure she wasn't missing anything. What she saw in there when she flicked the light switch made her drop the basket again. Sitting on top of one of Glizzy's Retro Jordan boxes was a red boot: her red boot. Well, Vy's red boot, but still, she was the one wearing it that night.

"Glizzy . . ." She eased her way into the closet and picked up the shoe. She didn't even know she had tears in her eyes until she held the boot to her chest. He'd kept it that whole time.

"I figured some time or other you'd come back for it. That's an expensive-ass shoe." Glizzy's voice sounded directly behind her. He was so close to her that she could feel the heat radiating from his body to hers.

"I don't know what you're talking about," Ava said, keeping her back to him.

"Yes, you do . . . Cinderella."

"Glizzy . . ." She tried to step away from him, but his strong arms wrapped tightly around her waist, and she couldn't move. No, it wasn't that she couldn't; she didn't want to.

"I knew it was you," he whispered in her ear, "the moment I heard your voice."

"How?" She cocked her neck, allowing his soft kisses access.

"Ever since the night I met you, your voice has been in my head. Your sweet, innocent voice. That and the boot were the only things I had to remember you by. I've known this whole time."

"Why didn't you say anything?"

"Because you didn't. I wasn't going to force you to reveal anything to me that you weren't ready to. Now, tell me." His strong, masculine hand traveled down her stomach all the way to the place between her legs. "Was that a nigga you were just on the phone with?"

"Nooo," she moaned softly as he squeezed his hand, triggering her clit to jump. "It was just my friend."

"Better have been," he told her and pulled her out of the closet.

"Glizzy, we can't." She turned to face him and pulled away. She shook her head and tried to think of the words to say so he could understand that anything between them was forbidden. "I'm—"

"What? The woman I'm in love with?" Glizzy grabbed her hands and kissed them with his soft lips. "That's another reason I didn't tell you that I knew who you were, ma because I needed to know if the feelings I had were real. But now I know they are. In this short time, I can't even go a day without being in your presence; and when I'm gone away from this house, I'm tryin'a rush business so I can get back to you before you run off again. You don't feel it?"

"Yes," Ava admitted and allowed herself to be pulled into him again. "Yes, Glizzy, I feel it. But I'm a maid and you're a prince. You make the messes; I clean them up."

"There's one mess that I can clean up if you let me."

His lips were on hers before she could muster another word. His deep kiss felt so good that any thoughts of fighting him off flew out of her mind. She wrapped her arms around his neck and allowed him to pick her up and lay her on the bed. It seemed like it only took seconds for him to completely undress her and throw her clothes to the side. He used the remote on the nightstand by his bed to dim the lights, and then he loomed over her, admiring every curve of her body. His fingers traced the stretch marks on her hips, and he licked his lips at the way her large brown nipples stared back up at him.

"You're beautiful, Ava," he whispered in awe. "More beautiful than I could ever have daydreamed. I'm going to make this pussy talk back to me, okay?"

"Okay," Ava whispered and opened her legs, giving him complete access. "Okay, Glizzy."

Her eyes fell on his erection through his shorts, and she felt her walls contract. It had been so long since she had let a man inside of her love cave that the mere thought of watching Glizzy slide in and out of her turned her on. She reached for him, and he came. She knew he wanted to taste her, but that would have to wait until the first round of him digging into her was over. Lips locked again, their hands explored each other's bodies. He broke their kiss so that he could lick and suck over her full breasts.

"Ohhh, Glizzy," she moaned, gripping the back of his head. Her fingers massaged his scalp as he mushed his face in between her breasts and kissed all over them. "Baby, I want you to fuck me right now. Please."

He removed his shorts and his boxers and positioned his tip right at her opening. Right before he slid into her wetness, he shook his head, teasing her.

"You coulda given me some of this wet-ass pussy a long time ago," he said, biting her nipples. "But instead you want to play like you didn't want me."

"Baby, I did want you. I was scared."

"Scared of what?" he asked. He sat up so that he could look her in the eye as he played with her. Slowly, he began sticking the tip of his ten inches of meat in and out of her pussy while rubbing her clit. Her body began jerking, and it turned him on immensely. "I said, scared of what?"

"I was scared that you wouldn't want me!" she cried out.

"Why wouldn't I want you?" he said, inching a little bit more inside of her. "You're smart."

"Unh!" Ava moaned, feeling his dick starting to tear her walls down.

"You're funny." Glizzy thrust harder that time, fighting against her tightness.

"Sssss!" Ava sucked her teeth and grabbed hold of her breasts, squeezing them for support.

"You're beautiful. And"—thrust—"I"—thrust—"love you."

He forced the rest of his shaft inside of her and welcomed her screams in his ears. Her face was twisted up in a grimace, but the way she rotated her hips, welcoming each thrust, let him know she was liking it. He put his hands behind her knees so that he could hold her legs up and watch his dick get swallowed by her fat pussy. He didn't think twice about hitting her raw. He would never disrespect her pussy by blocking the power it had with a condom.

Ava, too, wanted to watch. She opened her eyes and looked down at how good it looked sliding in and out of her.

"Oooh, baby," she said, throwing her pussy up at him to match his strokes. "I love you toooo!"

She began talking and saying things that she'd never said to any man as he continued to fuck her senseless. It got to the point where she could no longer match his strokes; she just had to take the dick.

"There it go," he said when he hit her G-spot and she tried to run. "Nah. You've done enough running for a lifetime. Take this dick."

"Oh! Oh! Oh! Oh!" she cried out whenever the tip of his dick hit her spot. She felt her clit swell up, and right before she released, her hands began to reach wildly for something, anything. "Baby. Babyyy! I'm about to cum! Glizzy, hold me!"

"Nah," he panted and pounded into her even harder. "Go crazy on this dick. I want to see. It's okay, Ava, you can go crazy on this dick."

And that she did. With him, she experienced an orgasm so powerful that her back arched an inch off the bed. It was like she was in an *Exorcist* movie, and the whole house had to hear her screaming Glizzy's name over and over. The sight was a beautiful one, and it turned him on to the point that he could no longer hold his own nut. He pulled out right before releasing inside of her and shot his nut on her chest. The plan had been to go for more than one round, but they were both so exhausted that all they had the energy to do was pass out and curl up under the blankets. They slept cuddled like that for hours, until it was time for Ava to get up.

The clock read ten minutes past eleven, and she knew that the time was now or never. She stood and dressed, watching Glizzy sleep. She had written a note of three words that she knew would break his heart when he woke in the morning:

Good-bye. I'm sorry.

***

She forced her feet to move; otherwise, she knew that she would never leave. She exited the room quietly and headed for her own. Once there, she showered quickly and then dressed in all black. She then put everything that she could in a backpack and grabbed her gun that she had tucked away underneath her mattress. By the time she was done with all of that, it was ten minutes to midnight. Ava kept her heartrate under control by not overthinking what was about to be done.

King Dex's bedroom was on the other end of the house. It was a task, but she managed to leave her room and make it all the way there without being detected. Working there for the short timeframe that she had, she'd learned the ins and outs of the security in place. She knew which ways each camera inside faced, and she knew where the guards went and didn't go at night. They never went into the main kitchen past ten; Whitney forbade it. Ava used that to her advantage and cut through it to get to the stairs that led upstairs. Checking the clock on her phone, she saw that the time read midnight, and she ducked behind the stairwell until she heard the guard in charge of standing outside of King Dex's door trudge down them. She held her breath as he walked by, but he didn't even think to look in her direction. Once he was gone, Ava figured she would only have about thirty seconds to get upstairs to his room before the next guard showed up.

She took the stairs two at a time, and when she got to his door, she quietly turned the knob in hopes of not waking him. Once she was inside, she shut the door behind her just as quietly. The room was dark, and the only light came from the moon shining through a window. She inched her way to the large bed where she could see his sleeping body. When she got to the bed, she aimed her gun at King Dex's head and prepared to avenge her mother's death.

"You made three mistakes."

The voice caught her off guard, and she squeezed the trigger of her gun, but nothing happened. She squeezed it again but, again, no shot rang out.

"That was your first mistake, hiding your gun in a place as obvious as under the mattress. I found that easily and removed the bullets. I commend you for infiltrating my home, but you are still an amateur. You don't even know what a gun feels like when it isn't loaded."

The lights flickered on, and Ava blinked, trying to adjust to the light. She saw King Dex in his pajamas, leaning casually on the wall next to the light switch. It was obvious then that he'd been watching her since she walked in the room. Her eyes flew to the bed and saw that she'd been caught with an okie-doke.

"Pillows," she gasped and looked back to King Dex with fear in her eyes.

"Your second mistake was not making sure that I was breathing." He stood up straight and walked slowly over to his tall wooden dresser.

Ava turned her body with him, not wanting him to be out of her sight. She was a gazelle in the lion's den, and she knew it was only a matter of time before he pounced.

"Your third mistake," he said, opening the top drawer of the dresser and pulling out a Glock 22, "was making my son fall in love with you. Now, normally I would just put two in your skull for all of the crimes you have committed. And, don't worry, Vy and the others will be next. But I have to know: why would you go through all of this trouble just to die?"

"You took someone I love away from me," Ava whispered with tears of fury mixed with terror running down her face. "You killed my mother."

"Who is your mother?" King Dex said, slowly loading his gun.

Ava wanted to run, but there would be no point. By then there was a guard on the other side of the door who would just catch her and take her right back to the devil himself. Ava felt her body grow weak. She had never been so frightened in her life. She'd let her rage get in the way of logic, and she completely forgot, until right then and there, that she was just a normal girl from Omaha, Nebraska, not a hitman.

"Alaya Dunning. Her boyfriend was a man named Dumphy."

"I thought so." King Dex smirked to himself and nodded his head.

"Why?" she asked, allowing herself to break down into sobs. "All of the blood . . . It was a massacre. My mom, she wouldn't hurt a fly. She didn't deserve to go like that."

"You must have known this was a suicide mission. Why would you even try?"

"Because even if I didn't kill you, you would kill me." Ava finally spoke her thoughts out loud.

"You would die for a dead woman?"

"She's my mother."

"Isn't she also the woman who put a man before you?"

Ava's eyes widened as King Dex approached her with the gun. "How do you know that?"

He didn't answer her. He put the cold steel to her temple and applied pressure to the trigger. Ava dropped to her knees and began to say her last prayers on earth.

She clenched her eyes shut and tried to erase the world around her, but somehow King Dex's voice still snuck through before he pulled the trigger.

"Tell me, how does it feel to know you did all of this for nothing?"

Chapter 10

"I know you're awake."

There it was: the voice that she'd been dreading since the day she was stolen away from her home. Lay Lay had no clue where she was, or why she was there. She was dirty, hungry, and thirsty, but no one seemed to care about that. The only thing that mattered to them was the thing that she could not tell them no matter how much she wanted to. Her wrists were shackled, and the chains were attached to the concrete wall of the basement she was in. She knew that it would only be a matter of time before they did her the way they did Dumphy.

"Are you ready to tell me where the money is, or are you still playing dumb?"

Lay Lay was sitting cross-legged with her back against the wall and with her arms in her lap. Her head was down, and her eyes were closed. She just wanted it all to be over. The basement that she was in was completely empty, besides the occasional rat that would come and keep her company. She honestly felt that the rats were coming and going just to see if she was dead yet and if they had some food. She opened her eyes and looked down at her hands, which were black and filthy like the rest of her body; and then she looked up at him.

"I told you already, Dorian, I don't know where the money is. Dumphy never told me."

Speaking just that one sentence seemed to take so much out of her. She hadn't eaten or had any water since the day she was taken. Her body trembled violently, and she clenched her eyes shut again when she saw him walk toward her in the dimly lit basement. He grabbed her by the chin and tightly squeezed the swelling that was already there. Lay Lay winced, but she did not cry out. She didn't have the energy, and she had started to welcome to pain.

"Dumphy was in your house every day, and the way he liked to run his mouth, there is no way that he didn't tell you."

"I told you all of the places that I think that he would put it. I just don't know any more. Dumphy . . ." Lay Lay hung her head and inhaled deeply. She paused for a second, and before speaking in a whisper, thought about everything Dumphy put her through. "Dumphy wasn't a good man to me. He could have twenty dollars while I had five, but still he'd take my five dollars. He took and took from me. My mistake was letting him. Yeah, I should have left him a long time ago. I was so scared of the thought of being alone that I didn't realize that I was already alone. I don't know where the money is. He was a selfish man. But, please"—that time the tears and sobs came as Lay Lay felt every word that came off of her tongue—"please don't let them come in here and hurt me anymore. I'm a good woman. The only person in this world I've hurt is the child who would give me the clothes off her back behind a man who has put me in the position to lose my life. Please don't let them hurt me anymore!"

Dorian let Lay Lay's chin go, but he did not stand up. He looked at the woman before him and took in the sight. In that moment, he did not view her as his enemy, but as a human being. He had not physically caused her pain, but the boys who were sent in to intimidate her had done damage. Her arms and legs had bruises on them that would take months to heal, and her jaw was probably broken from when Preston punched her in the face.

He remembered when they first pulled up to her home, how she was kicking Dumphy out, and he sighed. There was no woman on earth who would endure that much pain for a man she didn't even want anymore. She would have told him anything he wanted to know by now. The only reason she wouldn't have told was if she didn't know. He was sure that he'd taken many innocent lives in his time in the dope game, but hurting her was something he suddenly had no more desire to do.

He reached for his pocket, and Lay Lay jumped hard, but all he pulled out was a handkerchief from the pocket of his two-button suit. With it, he dotted the areas just under her eyes where the tears had hit.

"What are you doing?" she asked weakly.

"Absorbing the pain that I have caused you," he told her and pulled a set of keys from the same pocket. "Can you walk?"

"I don't know. I haven't tried. Are you going to kill me now? Since I don't know anything? If you do, please tell my daughter that I love her. And that I'm sorry."

"How about you tell her yourself?" Dorian freed her wrists and took notice of the cuts in her flesh caused by the tightness of the metal. Gently he placed an arm under her neck and another under her knees. "After you get some medical attention."

Epilogue

The day of the masquerade ball finally came, and Glizzy sat watching everyone around him have a good time. The entire building was packed, and the DJ was playing everyone's favorite songs back to back. It would go down as the party of the century. Too bad Glizzy wouldn't see it as such. He was dressed in all white from head to toe and even had a blinged-out diamond grill in his mouth and a gold crown on his head. Still, it didn't change the fact that the throne next to him was empty.

He still couldn't believe that Ava had up and vanished like that. That was something that he definitely did not see coming, and although he tried to cheer himself up, he could not get her out of his mind. He tried to search for her, but all of her social media sites had been taken down. It was like she had been erased from earth, and if you didn't know her prior, her existence . . . didn't exist. He didn't understand what had happened. What other reason, besides the fact that she was his Cinderella, did she have for coming to work in his home? It had to have been because she wanted him to find out who she really was. He didn't understand, but maybe it wasn't for him to understand. All he knew was that he loved her, and even though she had broken his heart, he hoped she was safe and happy, wherever she was.

In the midst of the party, King Dex was on the floor mingling with some heavy hitters. They had flown all the way from Detroit, and he decided why not partake in the festivities. He was in the middle of talking business when he caught his son milling around at his own event. He watched Glizzy for a moment, the younger version of himself. He always wanted his son to do what he wanted to do. He didn't have to follow in his dad's footsteps if he didn't want to, but, of course, he did, and King Dex let him. While Glizzy was under his wing, King Dex realized his son was a better man than he ever was, and if groomed correctly, he would be a better man than he ever could be. As Glizzy was his only child, his prince, King Dex might have spoiled him a little too much, especially in the absence of his mother, but he thought he did a pretty stand-up job raising him into a man.

Seeing Glizzy with such a long face did something to King Dex's spirit, and he excused himself so he could make his way over to the front of the ballroom. When he approached Glizzy, he placed his hand on Glizzy's shoulder and squeezed once gently.

"Son, why do I feel like you aren't enjoying yourself? Isn't this what you wanted?"

Glizzy shrugged his shoulders and fixed his diamond cuff links. "I guess."

King Dex, who wore an all-gold Armani suit, took a step back and put his hands in his pockets. He studied his son for a second and then chuckled to himself. "You aren't still upset about that cleaner running off, are you?"

"Why do you think that? I ain't stressing over no female."

"Good. I'm sure she was just another bitch, like the rest of them," King Dex said, laying the bait.

"She ain't no bitch," Glizzy snapped, and when he caught himself, he shook his head. "My bad, Pop."

"Talk to me, son," King Dex said. "Tell me how you feel. It's okay for grown men to have feelings."

"You don't."

"And what makes you think that?"

"I've seen you put a bullet in a man's throat in front of his daughter and tell her to clean it up."

"I did that?" King Dex said, trying to remember.

"See?" Glizzy shook his head yet again. "You wouldn't understand how I feel, and I ain't gon' let you clown me, either."

"Touché," King Dex said. "But just because I won't understand doesn't mean you should bottle it in. You've been moping around for a few days now, checking that phone whenever it vibrates, like the world depends on it. I may not know much about feelings, but I know when somebody is in love. You fell in love with that cleaning girl, didn't you?"

"She was more than that, Pop, but the way you go through women you wouldn't understand what one girl can mean to a man."

"I guess you are right." King Dex shrugged his shoulders. "I just hate to see you down like this. Not because I think it will affect your work ethic, but I don't want it to ruin how you view love, like your mother did for me."

"Pop."

"I'm serious. I know that's your mother, but she was a piece of work. She ruined love for me forever, and I will never let another woman get that close to me again because of her. Granted, you are my son, and I fashioned you in my image, but I want you to be a better man than I ever could be. You are already a better man than me."

"Thanks, Pop," Glizzy said. "I appreciate you for everything that you've done for me. And I thank you for throwing me this party, but saying all of that doesn't change the fact that she isn't here. Maybe you're right. Maybe she's just like the rest. I think I'ma head out early."

"No, son. You're going to miss the best part. I guess it was rude of me to call her just a cleaner." King Dex smiled mysteriously at Glizzy. "Especially when she is a real-life Cinderella."

At that moment, the music cut, and everyone turned to the entrance of the ballroom. At the top of the spiral staircase stood a beautiful woman wearing the most beautiful ballroom gown. The gown was a blue so light that it almost looked white. Her hair was pulled back, and her lips were a bright cherry red. Although the masquerade mask covered her face, Glizzy would recognize her eyes anywhere now. She was aided by none other than his housekeeper, Whitney, and another woman he'd never seen before. The smile on his face said it all.

"Cinderella," he said in a low voice, and King Dex gave a hearty laugh.

"Go on and get your happy ending, son," he said, accepting the hug Glizzy gave him.

As he watched his son run up the stairs and scoop the woman he loved in his arms, King Dex knew he made the right choice. He would never tell his son the tale of how he spared Ava's life for trying to take his. Most people viewed kingpins as ruthless and coldhearted, which was true. They could be that way to their enemies; but, even though she was ready to put a bullet in his skull, he could never view her as his enemy.

He had realized as she sat kneeling and praying that it was he who had become her enemy. He couldn't find it in his heart to kill the woman his son loved, nor could he kill her when he knew the only reason she was in that position was because she *thought* her mother was dead. So, instead of killing her that night, he set the gun down and embraced her the way he would have embraced a daughter if he had one. He told her that her mother's life had been spared as well, and he took her to the hospital.

Smiling to himself, he made his way through the crowd and back over to his guest of honor.

"She's pretty," a woman's voice said to him. "Who is she?"

"The girl who snuck into my room to kill me a few nights ago," King Dex said with a smile.

The woman's eyebrow shot up in humor, but King Dex stared at Ava in the distance. He had to admit, he liked her. He liked her a lot. He watched as his son and Ava were joined by three other young women and two boys, and he smiled to himself, recognizing them instantly.

"That, my dear Sadie, is a story for another time. Come." He held his arm out to the head of the Last Kings, the biggest underground drug cartel in the States, so she could grab it. "Let us go get some drinks and talk real business. Now, what was this you were telling me about?"

Before they walked away, King Dex turned back to look at Ava in the distance. She was looking back at him as well, and she placed a simple kiss on her fingers and then put her fingers to her chest. He shot her a fond smile and nodded his head before turning his head back to Sadie.

"Expansion," she said. "And a new drug."

That piqued his interest.

"I'm listening."

The End

Robin the Hood

Chapter 1

"Flip that couch!"

The voice barked with so much authority that all of the masked figures in the large living room jumped into action. The sounds of a family whimpering in a corner were hardly audible over the burglars ransacking the home. The Simpsons had been trying to have a nice, quiet dinner when they heard the knock on the door that would change their lives forever. Demetrius Simpson had opened the door not knowing that the masked figures on his doorstep were grim reapers coming to collect his soul. All of the bad business he had been doing in the streets of Omaha had finally caught up to him. He thought that by moving out west to a neighborhood where there weren't many blacks, he was saving himself. However, there was no nosey neighbor or gate that could stop what was coming for him.

"Please," he begged as his wife and children clung to him in the corner of their living room, "take whatever you want and leave. I have money upstairs in a safe!"

He wanted to get them away from his thousand-dollar couches. There was, in fact, $50,000 upstairs in the safe in his bedroom closet that they could have if they wanted it. One of the masked men stopped and approached Demetrius. Kneeling until he was at eye level with him, the masked man studied his sweaty face.

"Hmm," the deep voice grunted. He watched Demetrius cringe when the others pulled the pillows from the couch, and he saw even more beads of sweat form when they flipped open their switchblades. "Wait, y'all!"

"Man, what? We have a job to do!" one of the masked figures holding a switchblade said. His voice was slightly higher pitched, and he was the shortest of them all. His build was small, but it was always the little ones that you had to look out for. He had a crazed look in his bloodshot eyes, and they shifted from Demetrius to the man in front of him.

"Chill, bro," the one in front of Demetrius said. "He was just about to give me the combination to the safe upstairs." He turned back to Demetrius. "Now, you were saying?"

"Fifty-eight, twenty-four," Demetrius stammered and then rambled off the rest of the combination. "The master bedroom is straight down the hall off of the stairs."

The masked man in front of him nodded his head and then put a gun to the youngest of the two boys hanging on to their dad.

"If you're lying to me, I will kill him first." He stood up and nodded his head to the family. "Make sure he doesn't do anything stupid. I don't know which one of y'all left the rope and the tape behind, but I just want you to know how stupid you are."

With that he grabbed one of the bags they'd brought in and left, beginning his travels throughout the luxurious two-story house. His gloved hands were wrapped around the M16 rifle he had aimed and ready to unload if need be.

For the past ten years, Justin Hood had been a hired hitman, and he knew to always expect the unexpected. As he walked, he couldn't help but admire the home. It was at least 2,000 square feet, and if he could guess how much it was worth, he would say at least half a million dollars. In a state other than Nebraska, it would probably be worth triple that amount. If the money in the real estate business came in as fast as his current profession, he could definitely see himself wearing a suit, tie, and big, cheesy smile.

When he found the stairwell, he followed Demetrius's directions to the bedroom. Once in the spacious room, Justin shook his head. The man was living like a king off the heads of kids. The California king looked small in the room, and Justin made a mental note to hit the large walk-in closet before they left. On the soft, plush beige carpet, at the foot of the bed, was the fur of a lion, and on the walls were all types of tribal décor.

"This motherfucka really came up off that lick," Justin said out loud to himself as he made his way to the safe in the far corner of the room. "I hope he enjoyed all this shit while it lasted."

See, five years ago, Demetrius was just a soldier making runs for his boss, Arrik. Although he made good money, it would never be enough for a greedy man such as himself. He wanted more, and that hunger led him to do the faultiest thing he'd ever done: rob the hand that fed him. What Demetrius did to the young goons manning their posts in Arrik's trap house had been a gruesome massacre, mainly because they never saw the betrayal coming. Demetrius had always been someone they looked up to. They opened the doors to him because he was a trusted figure. One of the young men Demetrius murdered was Arrik's nephew and, if what he had done was already unforgivable, that kill crossed him over into the bad lands. Demetrius had gotten away with the souls of some of Arrik's most loyal, and $300,000 worth of his best heroin and coke.

Arrik chose not to retaliate in haste, and he allowed Demetrius to relish his lifestyle for months in his city. It had gotten to the point where the streets were calling him the next up for king, but Arrik had something else up his sleeve. He wanted to make sure that when he exacted his revenge, he would get triple what was stolen from him. When the time was right, he sought out the ones the streets called Shadow People. But, to him they were marauders: people who always got the deed done.

The job offered an amount of money that Justin would be a fool to pass up: $100,000 split five ways to get rid of the roach on Arrik's wall. Justin grinned to himself when he cracked open the safe and mentally added another $10,000 each to his team's earnings. Arrik had no clue about the fifty stacks in the safe, and what he didn't know wouldn't hurt him. Justin would bring him only what he asked for, nothing more and nothing less. He looked at it as a small fee for a service well done. Plus, he planned to split it equally with his whole team. After he loaded all of the money in the bag, he headed back downstairs.

"Yo, boss!" the same man with the high-pitched voice called when Justin entered the living room. "We found the coke! I guess that's why he ain't want us going near his couches." The couches had been cut open, and in front of his colleagues were at least fifty bricks.

Justin nodded his approval and pointed at the duffle bags on the floor. "Bag all that shit up, and then take whatever else it is in here that you want. You have ten minutes."

His team was so thorough they were done in five. One of Justin's rules for his team of bandits was to only take what could be carried. They never left a hit until every deed was done. He didn't want to risk going back and forth and being seen by the wrong set of eyes.

He'd gone back upstairs and stuffed into the last available duffle bag two Armani suits, a pair of Louboutins, three Rolex watches, and two pairs of gold cuff links. When they were ready to exit, Demetrius was still cowering in the corner with his family, watching them leave the house one by one. Justin made like he was about to leave as well, and behind him, he heard a cry of relief. Maybe they thought that the worst had been done but, if so, they were sadly mistaken.

Justin screwed the silencer on his gun and turned back to face them. "Do you know that not one of those boys you murdered was older than seventeen?" Justin asked in a low voice. "When you emptied that whole fifteen clip in Arrik's nephew's head, you never thought the surveillance footage would get back, did you? Well, Arrik sends you and your family his love."

The two young boys looked at Justin with confusion. He was sure that they didn't understand what was going on or why he was there. Justin's heart would have told him to let them live, but his heart had left a long time ago.

Pfft! Pfft! Pfft!

He showed no emotion at the blood splattering from the backs of their heads. Their necks snapped back from the force of the bullets entering their skulls. The precision of his aim was impeccable, and he knew they were gone before their bodies hit the ground. After he adjusted the straps of the duffle bags on his shoulder, he made his way out of the house. It was late, and the darkness shielded him as he ran to the white van parked around the corner. Once everyone was accounted for, they pulled off and headed in the direction of their hideout.

"That was an easy lick!" the driver of the vehicle said, removing the mask from his face.

"On God, Malik!" said the high-pitched voice, which belonged to Justin's trigger-happy shooter, Donte. He was sitting on Justin's right side, rummaging through the things he'd taken from the house. "I thought the nigga would at least put up a fight. He wasn't even strapped."

Tamar looked at Justin through the rearview mirror. Although he was the second youngest among them, his beard and mustache put many years on his physique. He technically wasn't even down with the crew; he was just a fill-in when he needed some extra money in his pocket. "Yo, boss man, was there really fifty bands in the safe upstairs? Or was the nigga jeffing about that to buy him more time?"

"Yeah, it's right here in this bag. We can divide it up equally at the spot and then head to Arrik's to get the rest of what's owed to us."

Donte and Malik nodded, excited about the fact that instead of $20,000 each, they would all get $30,000. Still, sometimes no amount of money could please everybody, and the next voice that sounded reminded Justin of that.

"How do we know there was only fifty thousand in the safe?" a deep baritone voice sounded from the seat in the back of the van. "Or that there wasn't more and you're trying to keep it all for yourself? We weren't up there with you. How do we know there wasn't one hundred thousand dollars in the safe?"

The flat tone belonged to Amos, a man from Memphis, Tennessee. He was new to the crew and, at first, Justin was reluctant to bring him into his circle. However, Amos could pick any lock no matter how big, small, or secure. At the time, that seemed like an essential talent to have in their line of work; however, lately, all of the questions that Amos had been asking were making Justin think he should have gone with his first instinct.

Before he could answer, a woman's voice spoke up: "The duffle bag is right there. Count it up if you feel like somebody is trying to cheat you."

The person in the passenger's seat removed the mask from her face, revealing a woman who gave meaning to the word "beauty." Her long, flowing hair fell on the sides of her face and rested on her shoulders.

Robin Hood, just like her brother Justin, was not a force to be trifled with. Over the years, her looks got her deemed a Lauren London look-alike, with her doe-shaped eyes, full lips, and high cheekbones. However, her attitude earned her a seat at the big boys' table. Just because she was pretty didn't mean that she was scared to get her hands a little dirty. At twenty-five, Robin was seven years younger than her older brother. When their parents died in a terrible car crash, Justin had taken her under his wing and taught her everything he knew. She learned to fight with precision and shoot a firearm without the voice of her conscience haunting her afterward.

Turning her head, she looked past Justin and directly into Amos's face. "Are you going to count it or not?" she asked when he did not make a move for the money.

Everyone was silent, waiting to see what would be the outcome of this exchange of words. The only sounds that could be heard were the gusts of wind coming through the slightly cracked windows of the van. Robin's and Amos's eyes were fixated on each other, and the two seemed to be in a war of who would blink first. After thirty seconds of glaring, Amos's face broke into a chuckle, and he shook his head.

"Nobody else wants to check and see for themselves?" he asked the other passengers.

"If Justin says there was only fifty thousand, there was only fifty thousand," Donte said, shrugging his shoulders. "That's my nigga, and I trust him. Either way, I came up tonight more than I thought I would. I don't care how much money is in that duffle. As long as I get what was promised to me, I'm straight."

"Right. Plus, Justin set up the hit and caught the bodies. Even if there was more money in there than fifty bands, he earned it."

Robin's eyes were still on Amos. She noticed the split-second look of displeasure cross his face right before it was replaced with another chuckle. She had the sudden urge to reach back and slap him, but he backed off.

"All right, I won't press the issue."

From the look on Robin's face, Justin could tell that she had something else to say. He shot her a look and shook his head at her. Her jaw tensed for a moment. Eventually, she turned back around in her seat, but not before shooting Amos one last dirty look.

Justin sighed and put his hood over his tapered fade. Leaning back in his seat, he closed his eyes, putting what had just taken place to the furthest part of his mind. They were always a little tense after a job, so he just chalked it up to that. All he knew was that he was tired and the moment they left Arrik's and got back to their safe house, he was crashing for a minimum of ten hours.

Chapter 2

"Mmmm, oh yesss, baby!" The sweetest moan bounced off of the four walls of the bedroom and back to Malik's ears.

"You like that shit, girl?" he asked, forcing her to arch her back deeper than it already was.

"Yes, daddy! I love this horse dick!"

Malik continued to plow into her from behind, throwing his head back and clenching his eyes shut. The way her pussy lips gripped his shaft had him feeling higher than the kush still circling around in his system. She caught each thrust like a good catcher was supposed to, and met him with some power of her own. His hands gripped her small waist, and the reason his eyes were clenched was because he couldn't handle the sight of his dick getting swallowed up by her fat ass and swollen womanhood. She was so wet that, mixed with her loud moans, there was a sound similar to a big pot of macaroni and cheese being stirred.

"I swear to God you got the best pussy, baby," he panted, not able to hold in the small moan that escaped his lips. "Damn, Robin! Bounce that shit back just like that!"

"I can't," Robin whimpered as she felt her clit swell up.

After the hit, Malik had offered to take Robin home when she said that she didn't want to sleep at the safe house with Justin and Donte. Amos ended up leaving as well, but he was the last thing on her mind. She knew what she and Malik were doing behind Justin's back was wrong, but she couldn't deny the feelings she had for Malik. Honestly, she couldn't explain her feelings for the man if she tried; she just knew that he lit a fire inside of her, one that made her want to jump his bones whenever she saw him. He gave her the best sex she'd ever had in her twenty-five years of life, and needless to say, she was hooked.

That night, the two booked a hotel suite and dumped money on top of the king-sized bed. There was something about fucking on top of thousands that did something for Robin's sexual drive. She loved the rough feeling of the paper against her naked body, and the bills comforted her when she needed something to grip while he was riding her—like right at that moment, when her love button exploded and her moans turned into screams.

"Cream all over daddy's dick." Malik encouraged her orgasm when he felt her buck in his grip. "Go ahead, baby. Daddy won't be mad at you. Just know I'm not done with you. I need three more."

Although he loved the feel of her juices flowing around his manhood, he would have rather had them on his face and his mouth. He flipped Robin over on her back with little effort, giving her the perfect view of his perfectly sculpted muscular frame. Her beautiful body was still quivering from the intensity of her orgasm, and she blinked her eyes rapidly to stop them from rolling in the back of her head.

"You want me to finish myself off?" he asked, stroking himself with his left hand and grabbing one of her succulent breasts with the other. He watched her perfect teeth bite her juicy bottom lip when he squeezed her nipple gently between his fingers. "I don't think you can handle another round."

"No, please give me more," Robin begged weakly, lifting her legs and opening them as wide as she could. "This is your pussy, baby. Take it. You can fuck me for however long you want, as hard as you want. You can hurt me and I won't tell you to stop. I promise. Just please make me cum again. Please, daddy, please!"

Malik watched Robin's hand slide down her flat stomach until it found what it was searching for. The purple chrome polish on her long acrylic nails looked even better as her hand softly slapped her sticky love box. He licked his full lips and felt his dick grow even harder in his hand. In the streets, Robin was the hardest chick you could find. She didn't play any games and didn't take shit from anybody. He would have never guessed that she was that submissive in the bedroom.

"I love how freaky you are, ma. Nasty-ass girl, you want me to fuck you again, huh?"

"Yessss."

"Well, I want to eat this pussy." He let her breast go and dived in face first.

His tongue was met with the taste of her sweet nectar, and he gripped her thighs so she couldn't run from him. She knew that to be a sign of him meaning business, and she gripped the bedsheets, trying to prepare for pure ecstasy. His tongue showed her clit no leniency, and with each lick, Robin's body jerked. Her hands found the back of his head and her fingers nestled in the soft curls of his high-top curly, tapered fade. She was scared to push his face deeper in her love box because she didn't know if she could take it, but she didn't want him to stop anytime soon. While her body shook and withered at his mercy, she silently thanked every woman who had come before her. They taught him the art of a woman's sex, and he mastered it. Malik licked, sucked, and kissed all over her sweet pussy until she had cum two more times in his mouth and his face was completely drenched.

That time, Malik didn't give her a chance to recuperate. Placing his strong hands behind her knees, he pushed her legs to the side of her face and stuffed his thick ten inches back inside of her. He knew she would have preferred for him to go slow until her orgasm subsided, but there was a fire inside of him that was screaming for him to pound her out.

"Ahhhh!" Robin hollered as a thin stream shot from between her legs and onto his stomach. "Malik! Malik, I can't take it, babyyy!"

"Yes, you can," Malik said while he gave her long, hard strokes. He leaned in so that he could place his mouth on hers and kiss her tenderly. "Take this dick. Take all this dick." He gave her five more good thrusts before slamming into her one last time.

"Shit!" he called out and squeezed her legs tight as he released his nut inside of her. He threw his head back at the intense feeling he was getting and closed his eyes so that he could relish it. "Damn, you got some good pussy, Robin."

"I know," she said with a breathy giggle. "That's why you can't stay away from me."

Malik pulled himself out of her and used the rest of his strength to lie down and pull her to his body. She grabbed the thicker cover that had gotten pushed to the end of the bed from all of their sexing, and she put it over their naked bodies.

"You are my kryptonite," Malik said, kissing the back of her ear as they spooned. "That pussy can get me killed. If Justin knew the things I did to you when the sun went down, homie would have my head on a stick."

Robin rolled her eyes at the far wall that she was facing. She hated when Malik subtly reminded her that, because of Justin, the two of them would never be anything but fuck buddies. Of course, she understood, but sometimes she wished that Malik would boss up and just tell Justin how he felt about her. "Why are you so scared of Justin?"

"I'm not scared of no man," he told her. "It's a respect thing. Dude has put me on to a lot of money. The last thing I want to do is throw in his face the fact that I'm fucking his little sister."

"I may be his little sister, but I am a grown woman. I can make my own decisions. We should just tell him."

She felt him grow stiff behind her, and she whipped her body around to face him. The first thing she noticed was the look of annoyance on his face and that his jaw was clenched.

"Malik, why can't we just tell him?"

"Because, ma," he said, sighing and wiping down his face with his hand, "that would be bad for business. And I fuck with you, but—"

"But?" Robin sat up in the bed and looked down at him with a raised eyebrow.

"But, it's not like I'm trying to be with you or nothing. You knew what this was from the jump, Robin. I told you when we first started this thing not to fall for me, and now look at you. Trying to get me to fuck up my money."

Just like that, his choice of words had Robin regretting being bent over with her ass in the air not even half an hour before. He had completely ruined the mood, and she was caught somewhere between being mad and being hurt. She was at a complete loss for words because never had she been in that position. She felt weak, like she had given somebody else power over her, and she didn't like it.

"Look," Malik said, reading her face, "it's obvious that you're upset. How about I just get my shit and go."

"It's four in the morning."

"What does that mean?" Malik asked rhetorically and got out of the bed.

Robin held the cover to her chest and watched him get fully dressed in less than three minutes. It was her money sprawled over the room, not his, so he didn't touch a single bill when he put his own duffle bag on his shoulder. After his white-and-black shell-toe Adidas were laced and his gun was tucked, he tried to lean in to give Robin a kiss, but she turned her head.

"Nigga, you're funny." Robin shook her head and waved her hand, dismissing him. "You can leave, and understand after this there is nothing but business between us."

"Man, all right." Malik stood upright and headed for the door.

He looked back at Robin when he got to the door, thinking that he would catch her glaring at him. Instead, he saw her staring sadly at her hands. Her long, disheveled hair hung loosely over her shoulders, and her back was hunched slightly. Oddly, it was the most beautiful he'd ever seen her. She looked so . . . vulnerable. A part of him wanted to go back to the bed and put her pieces back together, but an even bigger part of him reminded him that he could never give her what she wanted. Before he did something stupid, Malik turned his back on her and left the suite.

Chapter 3

"Daddy! Look at the fishies in the water!"

Arrik smiled as he watched his three-year-old daughter play by the man-made pond in the backyard of his three-story home. That summer day was a hot one, and he sat at the glass table that was positioned on his large concrete patio. A few of his partners sat at the table with him, and a few feet away they had the grill going. It was a mini-celebration for a successful hit the night before. That morning the news showed that a man by the name of Demetrius Simpson and his whole family were found slaughtered in his West Omaha home. The police had no leads on who had done the deed, and that was all Arrik needed to hear before he turned the television off.

He grabbed the Rémy bottle from the middle of the table and topped off his white Styrofoam cup. Holding the cup in the air, he looked around the table at his most trusted, and delegated a cheer.

"To snake-ass niggas being off the streets!"

"I second that!" Arrik's oldest friend, Roley, said with a smile on his face.

The two men had known each other since they were ten years old and had been thick as thieves ever since. Arrik was tall, muscular, and of Native American descent. He had smooth, honey brown skin that had a hint of red in it and a handsome square face; and he wore his thick, long hair in two Cherokee braids. He was what most girls called a "pretty boy," but there was nothing pretty about the ruthlessness in his heart. Roley, on the other hand, was only five foot seven, stocky, and wore his hair in a brush cut. He had full pink lips, and his skin and eyes were the same color brown. He was what most girls would deem "all right looking," but he kept himself up in the latest trendy gear and stayed with some ice on his body. The duo matched each other's fly, but most importantly they matched each other's loyalty.

After the table took their swig of Rémy, Roley nodded his head at Arrik. "So, what now? Now, since that greasy-ass nigga is off our streets, what's the next plan to level up? I know you got something up your sleeve. You been wearing that scheming look on your face all day!"

Arrik looked at Roley and grinned at how well his friend knew him. He shrugged his shoulders and continued to watch his daughter play for a few seconds before turning his attention back to the table.

"Ay, y'all, go make sure Naomi is straight, and one of y'all check the meat on the grill. If there's enough space, throw them shrimp on. I already put 'em on the skewers."

Arrik dismissed everyone at the table but Roley, and they already knew what time it was. The bosses had business to discuss, and Arrik kept everything on a need-to-know basis with his soldiers. He paid them well, so they never complained and always complied with his demands.

When it was just the two of them left at the table, Arrik faced Roley with a serious expression. "Yo, man, what's good? You lookin' at me like you got some bad news to tell me."

"Nah." Arrik shook his head. "Just some real shit. Some real serious shit."

"Nigga, please don't tell me you got another thot pregnant. I love my niece, but her mama is a straight ho, dog. I told yo' ass to stay out them strip clubs!"

"Chill," Arrik said, trying to keep a straight face. "I learned my lesson the last time. I don't have any more kids on the way. Not even a possibility."

And that was the truth. Arrik had been so busy handling his business it had been a while since he welcomed a woman to his bed. Naomi's mother, Malasia, had done a number on him, and ever since he had been unwilling to let another woman close to his heart. When he met her, the beautiful twenty-four-year-old was stacked the way he liked his women: fat ass, small waist, with a pussy so wet that he got caught slipping. One night of pleasure turned into a lifetime responsibility when she wound up pregnant.

He ignored all of Roley's warnings and took Malasia straight from the strip club and into his home. There was no way he could just leave her if she was carrying his seed. He was aware that many of the strippers at the club she was working at did recreational drugs. He told her that she would have to dead that immediately if she wanted to be his girl, which she claimed she did. He found out when she had their daughter one month prematurely that she was lying. Naomi was born with so much cocaine in her system that the doctors had no hope that she would make it. That was the day Arrik knew he was done with Malasia. He knew he didn't love her; he was forcing their relationship because of their child. He didn't have a father growing up, and he wanted to give his baby girl the sense of a two-parent home with two parents who loved her; however, seeing her lying in the NICU with all of those tubes in her body, he realized she only had one parent who cared.

His baby girl was a survivor. She made it through that first night, and every night after. It was not hard for Malasia's parental rights to be stripped and for Arrik to be granted full custody. Malasia didn't even put up a fight because the moment that she was stable enough, she skipped town. Arrik hadn't seen her since, and the last he heard was that she was back dancing at the same club he found her in.

"I'll never do that again. Hell nah." Arrik took another swig of his drink. "I learned my lesson from fucking with the most ratchet out of the crop. I will never get caught up like that again."

"So, what's the news then, boss?"

"Now that I have Demetrius handled, I can put my eyes back on the prize."

"And that is?"

"Expansion. Sadie ain't been too happy with me since them muhfuckas ran up in the spot and robbed me last winter. I was on pins and needles with her, but lately she's been liking the shit we been on. We've been pulling in and pushing out work like it's nothing. She feeling that shit."

"All right, what's the word then?"

"It's looking like we're setting up shop in Chicago, my guy."

"That's love!" Roley said with a big smile on his face. He was seeing money signs in his sights already. "Man, my nigga, I don't even know how you got in with them, but ever since we got plugged by the Last Kings, the revenue has been amazing."

Arrik's eyes became hazy for a second as he remembered what he did to gain Ray Thompson's trust. Blinking twice, he came back to and shrugged. "Shit, a nigga just had to stick and move."

Roley knew when not to press the issue with Arrik. Although he had always wanted to know how Arrik got them on with the Last Kings, he also knew it was something that his boy didn't want to talk about. He opted to change the subject in hopes of changing the mood.

"Speaking of sticking and moving, where is your boy at?" Roley checked the time on his phone and saw that it read ten minutes after one. "I thought he said he would be here at one."

Arrik too checked the time on his smartphone and saw that the guest of honor was late. Shortly after he had watched the news, he got an unexpected call with some interesting accusations. Normally, he wouldn't allow someone to come to where he laid his head, but under the circumstances, he made an exception. Plus, if there was any man willing to try to get through his security to harm him, more power to him. It was like Fort Knox all throughout his home.

"I guess what he needed to say wasn't that important," Arrik answered, but just as he was about to say something else, he looked up to see two of his soldiers coming around the side of his house.

They had somebody with them, a face that was familiar to Arrik, being that he had just done business with him. His soldiers stopped walking but allowed the man they had in tow to continue toward where Arrik was sitting. Their hands were on their waists, just in case the man tried anything funny. Arrik stood to his feet when the man got close enough to his table and then gave his soldiers a nod of dismissal, sending them back to their posts. The newcomer extended his hand to Arrik, who shook it firmly.

"Thank you for seeing me on such short notice, Arrik. This is a mighty fine place you have here."

"Thank you, Amos," Arrik said and motioned toward an empty seat. "Join us. We were just talkin' about how we didn't think you were going to show."

"I don't have any reason to fake," Amos said. "My day just got a little hectic, that's all."

"I understand that," Roley said. "As a man in the field, my days get hectic too. But one thing I have never been is late to a business meeting that I orchestrated."

"And you are?" It was obvious by Amos's tone that he didn't like the way he'd been addressed.

"I'm Roley. Nice to meet you."

Amos didn't return the words. Instead, he smoothed down his white Ralph Lauren T-shirt and pulled up his cargo shorts before sitting in the seat Arrik had indicated to him. When he did, Arrik followed suit and hopped right to business.

"Good work you and your team put in for me. I appreciate y'all for handling that for me. But, see, after the drop last night, I didn't think I would ever see any of your faces again. You said you have some information that is imperative to my business. What is it?"

Amos suddenly reached his hand in the deep pockets of his cargo pants, causing both Roley and Arrik to reach for their weapons. Amos did not pull out a gun, however. Instead, he pulled out two thick, crisp stacks of hundreds and tossed them to the middle of the table.

"Y'all got robbed last night," he said simply and leaned back in his chair. "There was an extra fifty thousand in the safe that Justin Hood didn't tell you about. When I asked him about it, he expressed his true feelings about you and your little operation, and let's just say he has no respect for you."

Arrik's jaw clenched as he stared at the money. Granted, he only asked to be brought Demetrius's product, but the fact that the extra currency wasn't even mentioned made him feel a type of way. Keeping his expression even, not wanting to see a gutter nigga like Amos see him sweat, Arrik leaned toward him and sneered.

"And I'm supposed to believe that you have some respect for me?"

"Believe what you want." Amos shrugged. "All I'm saying is that I see what you're doing here, and I like the way you move. Out of respect for your intake, I felt obligated to inform you of what was going on."

"Why? Are you tryin'a get put on or something?"

"Maybe, maybe not. You see, the money seen from being in my form of business is a gamble. It all depends on the job and, well, the jobs have been decreasing. They don't accommodate the type of lifestyle I have become accustomed to living. I need something that is going bring the currency in at a steady rate, and with that being said, I think that I would be an asset to you and your entire operation."

There was silence after Amos spoke, mostly because Arrik was trying to figure out if he was being serious. When nobody laughed, Arrik nodded his head.

"All right, but what can you do for or offer me to solidify your seat at my table? Did the bullets from your gun take the lives of Demetrius and his family?"

"Yes," Amos said without blinking. "Justin and the others were more worried about stuffing their bags with treasures than the job at hand. Me and my partner handled the job by ourselves, which is another reason why I felt slighted enough to come to you in the first place."

"Partner?"

The moment the word was out of his mouth, Arrik's security returned, that time with a new face in tow. Roley stood to his feet and removed the burner from his waist, looking with a displeased expression from Amos to the new guy.

"Who the fuck is this nigga? You were supposed to come alone."

"And I did," Amos replied to Roley. "We drove separate vehicles."

His smart remark almost cost him a bullet to the skull. Luckily, Arrik saved him.

"Who is he?" he asked, not yet allowing the new man clearance to approach the table.

"That's my mans. He helped me put in most of the work last night, and now he's here on the same shit that I'm on: redemption."

Arrik eyed the newcomer for a few moments before nodding his head. The security let him through, but that time they didn't go back to their posts. Instead, they kept their feet planted and kept their eyes on the table their boss was at.

"This is Malik," Amos told them before they could ask. "Malik, these are the gentlemen Justin wouldn't let us come and meet last night when he made the drop-off."

"Now I understand why," Malik said, holding his hand out for Roley shake. "This is a nice spot y'all have here. One day maybe I'll be able to afford one just like it."

Malik completely ignored the fact that Roley was pointing a gun at him. He figured if he was that hell-bent on using it, he would have already popped off. He kept his hand out until, finally, Roley lowered the gun slowly and shook it.

"Roley," he said, introducing himself. "I would say it's nice to meet you, but your boy hasn't yet told me what it is you two can offer us."

"Sounds like Amos." Malik smirked and shook his head at Amos. "It took me almost an hour to find this spot, and you still haven't gotten to the point. See, Amos here can open any lock known to man within five minutes."

"Three," Amos corrected him.

"Excuse me, three. And I"—Malik chuckled—"well, I know where I can lead you to five million dollars' worth of diamonds."

That piqued Arrik's interest. He looked at Roley, who also seemed interested, and then looked back to Malik. He contemplated his next move in his head while taking another swig of his drink. That was a lot of diamonds, and in the right market, he was sure he could make ten times the amount.

"Why can't you two get them yourselves?" Arrik finally asked. "You come into my home speaking about fifty bands, and now the talk is five mil. What's the catch?"

"No catch," Malik told him. "We are all businessmen here, and as a businessman, I know for a fact that there is no point moving in a city where another king already resides. The thing is, I don't care about being king, as long as I have the king on my side. That's good enough for me. The thing is, you have the connects, and it ain't no secret that you been on pins and needles with the Last Kings with all that Demetrius shit. That nigga had you looking like a baby boy, not a monster."

"You don't know shit about me, my nigga, so don't speak like you do." Arrik's growl was full of contempt, and it made Malik switch his approach to the situation.

"Look, I'm not on any disrespect. All I'm saying is I have a way for you to secure a quick bag, and with that money, you can cop whatever you need to from them to let them know you ain't hurting no more. With two million dollars' worth of diamonds, it will be like Demetrius never existed."

"I want half," Arrik said sharply.

"What?"

"You said two million, but I want half of the five. The extra five hundred thousand is my fee for my services. If you can't do that, you can leave, and we can act like this conversation never happened."

Arrik watched Malik's jaw clench ever so slightly as he pondered over what he would say next. His eyes never left Malik's, and finally, after almost three minutes, Malik nodded his head.

"Deal, but the shit has to be foolproof. I need your most trained killers on this one."

"Who did you say had these diamonds again?" Arrik asked, curious about Malik's request.

"Justin Hood."

Chapter 4

Fwap! Fwap! Fwap!

Justin sat at the edge of his bed, thumbing through a big stack of hundred-dollar bills. A week had passed since the incident at Demetrius's home, and since then, he had been on a few more jobs. He finally had some downtime, and he wanted to indulge in his favorite hobby: sex. In front of him, dancing buck-naked, were two strippers by the name of Sweet Tea and Coffee, and they were *very* familiar with Justin. Whenever he called the club to hire two private dancers, those two were always his first pick.

Coffee was a chocolatey delicious woman who wore colorful wigs while on the clock. That night she had opted for a purple so bright you couldn't miss her. Coffee was so thick in the thighs and backside that a person didn't even notice that she was just average in the face. Her makeup put her at a complete ten, but without it, she was a solid six. Her breasts were small but perky, and she had a small stomach that Justin enjoyed licking all over.

Sweet Tea was a brown-skinned, voluptuous woman with a small waist. Her fine hair was cut into a pixie cut, and Justin noticed that she must have gotten it colored red since the last time he saw her. She was one of the most beautiful women Justin had ever laid eyes on, but he would never pursue her. Her full lips were perfect for sucking dick, and her second set of fat lips were perfect for taking it.

While Coffee was busy bouncing her ass and bending over so he would have the perfect view of her pink pussy, Sweet Tea couldn't wait any longer. She approached Justin, who sat in nothing but his boxers on the bed, and she took the money from him, setting it to the side.

"The money is a bonus," she whispered in his ear right before she mounted him. "You wanna know the real reason I love coming here?"

"What's that?" Justin asked, taking two big palmfuls of her ass in his hands.

"This big-ass dick," she said and ground down on his rock-hard manhood. She moaned as it rubbed against her clit and she bit her lip. "I be missing how you feel inside of me, baby. Nobody makes me cum the way you do."

Justin chuckled to himself before leaning his head and flicking his tongue across her right nipple. He didn't care about anything she was talking about at the moment. She didn't have to say all that she was saying; regardless, the money was hers. The only reason they were there was for him to get his dick wet. Justin by no means was the type of man who needed to pay for pussy; it was just easier that way. He didn't have time for any woman to be falling in love with him because he knew he wasn't ready for love. A woman would demand too much of his time, time he didn't have nor was willing to spare. He liked the fact that Sweet Tea and Coffee came with a "no strings attached" contract. They were there strictly for him to get his dick wet and then they were gone. Right then, however, Sweet Tea was blowing his high.

"Shut up," he told her. "I don't care about all of that. I just want you to take this dick. Can you do that for me?"

Surprisingly, his words didn't anger Sweet Tea; they turned her on. She loved the gutter in him and wished like hell she could be the bitch on his arm. But men like him just didn't want that, so she would give him what he wanted. She pulled his thick, long shaft from his boxers and began to slide it up and down between her moist pussy lips. While she did that, she poked her chest out even more so that he would have easier access to her breasts. She was already high as a kite, being that she and Coffee had smoked in the car before they pulled up to Justin's three-story home, and his tongue was just uplifting her even more.

"Ooooh, Justin!" she squealed over and over whenever the tip of his dick hit her enlarged clit. "Yessss! Suck my titties just like that, baby. Just like that."

"Hold up," Justin said when he couldn't wait any longer. He held on to Sweet Tea's lower back as he reached for his nightstand. From it he pulled a box of condoms, knowing it was going to be a long night of sexing. After ripping one open, he made Sweet Tea stand up so that he could take his boxers completely off and put it on. Right before he pulled Sweet Tea back onto him, he used his fingers to tease her love box. "This is tonight's disclaimer: a nigga been under a lot of stress lately, so I have no other plans than to fuck the shit out of both of you tonight. If I hurt your pussies, I'm putting this dick in your ass. If I hurt your ass, then I'm shoving it down your throats. Coffee, get on the bed and play with that pussy while I fuck Sweet Tea. Don't worry, I'ma save some dick for you too."

He didn't even wait for Coffee to obey his command before he grabbed Sweet Tea by the waist and slammed her down on his erection. He awakened every sense her walls had, and her initial scream solidified that. She wasn't afraid of the dick, though. Although he led the pound game, she rode him with expertise and met every upward thrust he gave her with a downward drop of her own. She was slippery, just the way he liked it, and he enjoyed that her pussy was tenured. It meant that he could plummet into her and didn't have to hold back because she couldn't take it. He was able to enjoy her at any depth he chose.

The two of them were so deep into their sexing that neither noticed the bed dip slightly when Coffee climbed on. She was positioned up by the headboard with a pillow at her back for support. Her fingers were between her legs as she watched Justin put a hurting on her friend. In all honesty, she was paying more attention to the way Sweet Tea's breasts were bouncing up and down, and getting turned on. Quiet as it was kept, Coffee thoroughly enjoyed the type of jobs where she would get to play with Sweet Tea's assets. No, she wasn't a lesbian by any means, but Sweet Tea turned her on the way nobody else could. She liked being able to do what she couldn't do at the club without all of the other girls being in her business. Coffee couldn't wait for Justin to get done with Sweet Tea so she could have her way with her pussy.

"Oooh." The moan slipped through Coffee's lips as she released her sticky juices in her hand. "Damnnn. Sweet Tea, come lick my pussy while he hits you from the back or something. My shit is throbbing for some attention."

Justin ground into Sweet Tea one last time before he let her up on shaky legs. He helped her balance herself so she could climb on the bed and crawl to where Coffee sat. Before she could get one lick in on her own, Justin's hand was on the back of her neck. He mushed her face into Coffee's already wet opening while he played with her chocolatey nipples. When Coffee's eyes began to roll to the back of her head, he removed the condom from his erection and let Sweet Tea's neck go so he could grab Coffee's face. She already knew what was coming and had her mouth open wide to receive his delicious penis. She sucked and slurped all over it, the way that he liked, until he threw his head back.

"Shit!" he said and gripped her face even tighter so that he could fuck her throat. He forced the tip of his manhood to the back of her throat and felt it contracting around his shaft. "Yeah, suck this dick, you nasty slut. Suck this shit like you ain't even gon' get any more dick in your life. Yeah, just like that."

"Fuck her," Sweet Tea told him seductively while kissing Coffee's clit. "She wants some dick. I can tell by how her clit keeps jumping. Bend her over so I can watch."

Normally Justin didn't like being told what to do, but what Sweet Tea had just proposed didn't sound like too bad of an idea. He grabbed another condom, and by the time it was on, Coffee was already in the "face down, ass up" position. He licked his lips at how wet her fat cat was. Sweet Tea was on her back with her legs up in the air, working her middle finger in and out of her love canal. Watching her and sliding into Coffee at the same time let him know that his first nut was soon to come, but that meant nothing to him. He had a whole box of condoms to finish off that night.

Robin ran up the stairs of the house that she and her older brother shared. Already dressed in a pair of gray joggers and a tank top, she headed directly for Justin's room to see if he would do some combat training with her. When she got to the door, she instantly stopped her hand mid-knock.

"Ohhh, Justin! Daddy, that dick feels *soooo* good in my pussy! Please don't . . . don't stop."

Robin's face twisted up in the most disgusted face that she could muster. The last thing that she wanted to do was walk in on her brother having sex, so she was happy that she hadn't just burst into his room the way she usually did. She heard a second voice moan his name, and she knew instantly who he had in his room.

She rolled her eyes and backed away from the door so that Justin could continue to tear Coffee and Sweet Tea down.

"This nigga would choose the day that I need to let off some steam to have these hoes come over."

She hated that Justin would let women of their status into their home, although she knew she had no business looking down on anybody, because nobody should have technically trusted her in their home. However, the difference was she didn't look like it, while they looked like they couldn't be trusted. She was just glad that Justin never let them stay the night, and she was even more glad for the cameras they had throughout their home. Sighing, she decided to head to the basement of the house by herself since there was no telling when he would be done entertaining his guests.

Their entire basement was set up exactly like a gym facility, but Robin had no interest in using any of the machines. She walked past the treadmill and the ellipti-cal, not stopping until she got to the punching bag. To the right of the punching bag was the large matted workout floor that she and Justin fought on. Sitting down, she did her stretches to ensure that she would not pull any muscles from the strenuous workout she was about to put herself through. She was ready to put a hurting on her own body, because that was the only pain she could control. Lately, things around her had been spiraling in a downward motion. She reflected on the day their parents died. It was also the first day she picked up a gun.

Seventeen-year-old Robin Hood sat in the front office of North High School as she waited for her father to come and pick her up. She knew he wasn't going to be happy when he saw her, especially given the reason he had to come and get her. It was no secret that Robin's behavior at school was less than satisfactory. Her teachers treated her like she didn't matter, so she acted accordingly. Bad days were common for her, and that day was worse than most.

Robin didn't have everything the other girls had. Although both of her parents worked, they just didn't have the extra money to buy her in-style clothes or name-brand shoes, so she got what she got. She grew tired of constantly being picked on for lack of material things and being pointed out as the bad guy when she defended herself. Eventually, it got to the point where she didn't care anymore, and anybody who disrespected her would have to pay.

"I had high hopes for you," Principal Atkins said to her, shaking his head in her direction. He was a short black man with a bald head and a mustache. "I can't believe you would do something like this when you are so close to graduating." "This" was the fact that she had beat another student so badly that her jaw cracked.

Robin shrugged her shoulders, letting Principal Atkins know that she didn't care about what he was talking about. The staff in the school let the students treat her any kind of way, and they only wanted to jump into action when she retaliated, so in her mind, it was fuck them.

"Makayla is a bitch, and she shouldn't have said what she said about my mother. If she would have watched her mouth, I wouldn't have hit her in it."

"Words are just words, Miss Hood."

"Oh, really? So, it's okay that she told me that if my mother sold some pussy, then she would be able to buy me better clothes?" Robin leaned back in the chair she was sitting in and looked him square in the eyes. "If that is the case, why did you suspend me for three days a few weeks ago for telling Jessica Sams that she was a whore who sucked too much dick? Those were just words too.

Oh, and let's not forget that the only reason I said that was because she stole my underwear from my gym locker after class."

Principal Atkins seemed to be at a loss for words after her statement, just like she thought he would be. She rolled her eyes at him and scoffed in pity. He was a sellout. It wasn't a secret that the staff didn't like her, and the only reason she could think of had to do with her older brother, Justin Hood.

"It's okay that none of the teachers and you don't like me." Robin glared at him. "But you shouldn't make it so obvious."

"Robin—"

"Stop fucking talking to me," she snapped and put the hood of her sweatshirt over her head. "I'm done with this conversation. Just tell me when my dad gets here."

"He's not coming. I came instead."

She heard the voice and instantly looked for the owner of it. There, standing in the doorway of Principal Atkins' office, was a face that was the spitting image of her own. It had been a few months since Robin last saw her older brother, and her insides erupted with happiness.

"Brother!" she squealed as she jumped up from her seat to embrace him. "What are you doing here?"

"I was going to surprise you when you got home, but I overheard Principal Atkins call Dad for you. Told him I'd come scoop you up right quick."

"I really would have liked for your father to come." Principal Atkins interrupted the family reunion. "She put a girl in the hospital."

"She should have watched her mouth," Justin responded, not giving the principal eye contact. He studied his sister's face and noticed that she had a few scratches there, and he shook his head. "You let her get close enough to touch your face? I know I taught you better than that."

"Figures that you would be the one promoting this kind of behavior," Principal Atkins scoffed, standing to his feet. Compared to Justin's tall frame, he was a little man, but that still didn't stop him from speaking his mind. "You were no good when you went to this school, and you're no good now. I know all about what you're doing out there in them streets, boy, and if you don't slow it down, there is no doubt in my mind that you'll be in a jail cell soon."

"Don't talk to him like that."

"Shut up!" Principal Atkins snapped. He'd had enough of being disrespected in his office for one day and wouldn't stand for it any further. "You are suspended until further notice! There is no place for trash like you in this school!"

Robin's face dropped, and Justin's jaw clenched. He put his hands in the pockets of his designer jeans and finally made eye contact with the bold-talking principal.

"You haven't changed a bit, Reginald," Justin said, calling him by his first name. "Still a man who thinks his job title is his protection. Since you supposedly know what I'm doing out there, then you know how I get down. Bowie Drive. You live there with your wife, Adessa, and your two small children. You have a dog, a black lab, and betta fish named Charlie and Charlie Two. Right now, your wife is home alone with the kids feeling safe because you have an alarm system. Those things are so faulty; you see, they go off for a whole sixty seconds before they alert anyone there is something wrong. By then, the niggas I send to run up in there would have already slit her throat and put two bullets in the brats' skulls."

Principal Atkins was a brown-skinned man, but at Justin's words, his entire complexion flushed. He swallowed hard as his eyes darted from Robin and then to Justin as if he were looking at two creatures not from this earth. Even Robin had to admit she felt icy from Justin's cold words, and she knew he meant everything he'd said.

Justin stood there, looming over Principal Atkins, silently daring him to speak another word. When he did nothing but stammer and sit back down at his desk, Justin turned his back on him.

"She'll be here tomorrow, and I don't want to hear about any other issues when it comes to my sister, understood?"

"Understood," Principal Atkins said in a barely audible voice. "I'll see you tomorrow then, Robin."

Robin flicked him off and followed her brother out of the school. What an odd twosome they must have looked like walking side by side. Although they were the spitting image of each other, it looked like the prince and the pauper, like they lived two completely different lives. They did, but it had not always been like that. Robin knew that their parents' lack of money was why Justin dropped out of high school his own senior year. She also knew that was why he decided to get in the streets. She never looked at him differently for it; instead, she respected him, and in a way, she envied him.

"Dad really let you come get me?" Robin asked curiously when they got in Justin's 2009 Mustang. "He must really be fed up with me."

"Nah," Justin said, pulling out of the school parking lot and turning onto Ames Street. "He was fed up a long time ago when I went to this school. He's just an old man going through the motions of having two bad-ass kids."

Robin couldn't help but laugh. She was so happy that her brother was in town. There was no one else in the world who understood her the way he did. The two of them had always had a tight bond, and the longest they'd ever been apart was when Justin decided to move out of the house. He never told them where he was living; he would just say that he'd be around if they needed him.

She studied him as he drove toward their parents' house on Bedford and couldn't help but replay in her head his words to the principal. "You were serious back there, weren't you?" she asked finally.

Justin had been lost in his own thoughts when her voice sounded. He took his eyes off of the road to face her, and he knew exactly what she was asking. A part of him wanted to tell her that he was just trying to scare the man, but he had never lied to his little sister before, so he wasn't going to start. "Yeah."

"You really have people who would do that for you?"

"Do what?"

"Kill for you."

"Yes."

"What is it that you do exactly?" she asked like she always did.

His normal answer was always, "I move around and get money." And that's what she honestly expected him to say, but that day he shocked her.

"You really want to know?"

"I wouldn't have asked if I didn't," she told him.

"Have you ever wondered why Mom and Dad never accept my money, no matter how much I offer to give them?"

"I never knew that you offered to give them money."

Justin looked over at her and looked her up and down with a raised eyebrow. "Do you think I would ever willingly let you walk around looking like that without trying to help you out? Mom and Dad ain't never accepted my money or my gifts for you."

"Why?"

"Because they say that the money is dirty and they want no part of it."

"Well, is it dirty?"

"It just depends on the stance you are taking when you're looking at it. To me, no, it isn't. It's as clean as a whistle. But others might look at it as dirty as a toilet seat."

"Do you sell drugs, Justin?"

"No," Justin said with a straight face. "I'm a bandit. I rob people, and I sometimes kill them."

Robin stared at him to see if he was serious, and after seventeen years of being his sister, she could tell that he was as serious as a heart attack. She was quiet for a while, not knowing what to say. She swallowed the saliva that had built up in her mouth, and she looked out of the window.

"You scared of me now?"

"No," she said, still looking out the window. "You're my brother. I could never be scared of you. I'm just mad that our parents have me walking around dusty in Payless shoes when I don't have to be."

"Might as well have put you in some light-up shoes," Justin joked and put a grin on Robin's face.

"Shut up. But for real, though, I can't believe them."

"They're just doing what they feel is best for you," Justin said as he turned down the street they lived on. "Can't do nothing but respect it. They may not be able to give you the material things that you want, but you have to be grateful for all that you have. Not having what you want just fuels you to go get it yourself in life. No matter what you do, they'll be proud. I wish I could say the same about me."

"Yeah." Robin playfully nudged him with her shoulder. "Out of the two of us, you're definitely the screwup."

"Forget you," he told her. "Since I'm so screwed up, how about we say forget the shopping spree I cleared with our parents to take you on?"

"Wait! Wait! I was just playing!"

She was still giggling when they pulled up to the three-bedroom, two-story cookie-cutter house. Robin called it a cookie-cutter house because five people on the same block had the same house. In the driveway of their home, she noticed a car that she'd never seen before, and she furrowed her brow. Her parents had never been the type of people to have company. They always hated for people to know where they lived.

"Who's that?"

Justin shrugged his shoulders as he too eyed the red Buick. *"They weren't here when I left,"* he said as he leaned forward in the driver's seat and studied the house. *"The curtains in the living room are shut, too. Stay here real fast."*

"Justin?" Robin asked when she saw her brother put his hand to his waist before getting out of the car. *"What's going on?"*

"I'm probably tripping. But just stay here and lock the doors, okay? I'll be right back."

But he didn't come right back. As soon as he stepped foot in the house, Robin heard the shouting begin. She heard more than that, actually. Things in the house were being broken, and when the gunshots sounded, she jumped violently in her seat. Her hands were trembling because she did not know what was going on. Where were her parents? Was Justin okay?

Although he had told her to stay in the car, she couldn't. She opened the car door and hightailed it to the entrance of the house. The first thing she saw was blood splattered on the walls and on the floor. She didn't know whose blood it was, and she prayed it wasn't one of her family members'.

"Mom?" she called as she made her way up the stairs of the house toward the living room. *"Dad? Justin?"*

Nobody answered her. She walked slowly until she got to the top of the stairs and made a quick left into the living room. What she saw made her scream instantly.

"Oh, my God! No, no, no, no, no."

The sight caused her to shake her head, numb, and repeat the same word over and over. There, bound to two of the wooden chairs from their dining room set, were her parents. Only thing was, they weren't her parents anymore. They were dead, throats slit ear to ear. Sitting on the carpet, with a still-smoking gun in his hand, was Justin. A few feet away from him was a man, around his age, with a bullet in his forehead and another in his face. The gun was hanging loosely as Justin stared at his parents' lifeless bodies.

"He killed them," he spoke in a hoarse voice. "They're dead. They're dead, and it's all my fault."

The dead man on the ground was Bruno Maxwell. Justin had told Robin the truth when he said he was a burglar. He, however, left out the fact that he was also a hired hand. A few months back, he was hired for a job in Texas that had gone successfully. His job was to kill his target, Brandon Maxwell, which he did easily and also took a few of his most precious belongings. His one mistake had now come back to bite him in the ass.

The night he was sent to do the job, Brandon's younger brother had been in the home. Justin spared his life for the simple fact that, if the tables had been turned, he would want someone to spare Robin. That was a decision he would now regret for the rest of his life. Bruno must have been following him for a long time and had finally decided to exact his revenge.

"This is all my fault," he said again, that time feeling a sob well up in the back of his throat. "Go grab whatever you can. You have to come with me. We can't stay here."

Although all Robin wanted to do was fall to the ground and curl up in a fetal position, she did what she was told. Her hands were shaking violently as she stuffed as many clothes as she could into a duffle bag. When she came back into the living room, she saw that Justin had covered both of their parents' bodies with a bedsheet, and he had tears streaming down his face.

When he saw Robin staring at him with hollow eyes, he knew her life had been changed forever. He was all she had left, and that was because of him. In the blink of an eye, she had lost everything, and he knew that it was his job to give it back to her. His gun was already tucked away again. Right then and there, he made the decision to never lose another person he loved. Especially not his sister. He wanted to hold her and tell her that everything would be all right, but when he opened his mouth, she shook her head.

"If the gun you killed him with isn't registered, then we have to get out of here. They'll take you and . . . and I can't lose you too."

"You won't." Justin walked up to her and pressed her head to his chest. "I promise you won't ever lose me. I have some people who are already on their way to clean this up. It's still a workday, so I doubt anybody heard the gunshots. Let's go."

He took the bag from her and shielded her eyes so she wouldn't see the blood seeping through the white sheets or the body on the ground anymore. As soon as they were in the car and pulling away from the murder scene, a white van was pulling up. Justin sped off in the direction of the Doubletree that he was staying in downtown. His heart was empty, and when he looked at his sister, he could tell hers was too. She had learned firsthand with sight and experience that the world was not black and white. It was bloody red.

A few days later, the home that she was raised in was found burned to the ground. The deaths of Rhonda and Mark Hood made the news, but it was said that they died in the house fire. No one ever found out what really happened to them, and it wasn't until after the incident that Robin realized that she didn't get any of their old family photos from the house. Her parents were literally only memories, only to be remembered in her dreams.

Robin snapped back to reality and finished her stretches. She remembered like yesterday the way Justin kept sneaking glances at her in the car. He felt guilty and responsible for their parents' deaths. But, no matter how angry Robin was, she would never be angry at him. The universe worked in mysterious ways, and even then she knew that every happening had a reason. Then, she might have felt like nothing would be the same anymore; and, as time passed, she found that she was right.

She grew used to it, and instead of hiding from it, she welcomed her new life. After their parents were killed, Justin moved back to Omaha to ensure that Robin graduated from high school, unlike him. But, afterward, very much like him, she wasn't excited for the college life or even trying to apply for a job. She was attracted to fast money, and she asked Justin to teach her everything he knew. It amazed her that her brother would leave town for a weekend and come back with no less than $15,000 each trip. The house that he paid cash for was one that she never dreamed she would be able to live in, and that solidified his moves more than anything else. She appreciated him for everything that he did for her, but she was grown. She was tired of him taking care of her and giving her an allowance like he was her parent. Robin was ready to move around and get to the money on her own. At first, he was against it, saying that what he did was just too dangerous for her.

"Not if you teach me," she had told him. "The only thing in this world that I was ever afraid of was losing my parents, and that already happened. So now I feel like there is nothing holding me back from anything."

Those words were what made him change his mind; plus, he knew that she wasn't going to let up anytime soon. She had no idea then, but her brother would train her to be a war machine. Her name would soon ring bells in the underground with both fear and respect attached.

Getting to her feet, she went to the punching bag to let off some of her built-up steam. Both her and Justin's boxing gloves were hung up side by side, hers red and his black. She almost started the workout without the gloves at all, but she knew she wouldn't hear the end of Justin's chastising if she did so. After she wrapped her hands, she stuck her hands in her custom-made boxing gloves and pounced around the punching bag.

Granted, she loved the life her brother had built for her, and she would forever be grateful; however, she was ready to just settle down and live comfortably for once. It seemed like if they weren't on a job, they were preparing for one. When she had asked to be a part of Justin's world, she didn't think that it would completely consume hers. She felt as if she was losing her sense of self, and maybe that was why she had started to cling harder to Malik. He was her only getaway from the world as she knew it, but she had to ask herself, if he weren't so accessible, would he even be her type? The way he had acted the last time they were together really was weighing heavily on her shoulders. He didn't want her, not in that way anyway, but if he did, would she really want to be with him? She felt that maybe she was so invested in him because he was the first man besides Justin she'd opened up to. She felt like she owed it to herself to at least try to see where it went, but where did she want it to go?

Her thoughts plagued her mind with confusion. Her body moved on its own, and by the time she was done beating up the punching bag, her entire body was drenched in sweat. She didn't know how much time had passed, but when she trudged back up the stairs, she heard giggling in the kitchen that the basement door was off of. When she emerged from the basement, she saw who the giggles belonged to. There, sitting their practically naked asses on her clean beechwood counters, were Coffee and Sweet Tea. She had to pause and turn around, for a second. After she blinked her eyes to clear her vision, because she had to be tripping, she turned back around hoping to see a different view. It was the same.

"Now, I know good and damn well y'all don't have your nasty and trifling asses on my counters!"

Coffee, who had been in the middle of telling Sweet Tea something, shot daggers toward the basement door. Her dirty look was meant for the owner of the voice, but when she saw the owner was Robin, she quickly fixed her face.

"My bad, Rob. We trippin'!" She tried laughing to play it off. "You know we're a little tipsy. Your brother had us up there working us out. Okay?" She and Sweet Tea shared a laugh, but they got off the counter.

"I don't want to hear about what my brother did to you, okay?" Robin mocked them. "I just want to know when you're leaving because y'all are stinking up my house."

"We aren't leaving until the morning," Sweet Tea told her with a slight neck roll, "because Justin said we could stay."

"Justin said what?" Robin said, giving them an incredulous look. "Aw, nah, y'all got to get up out of here before then."

"Yo, Robin, why you trippin'?" Justin entered the kitchen while putting a white Ralph Lauren T-shirt over his muscular body. By the way he walked, it was obvious that he was tired, but that didn't stop Sweet Tea from looking at him like he was a snack.

"You took a shower already, baby?" she asked with a pout. "But I like you when you're sticky."

Robin pretended to throw up in her mouth. She could have punched her brother in his neck, and the glare she was giving him told him how badly she wanted to. She pointed at the women and shook her head. "They can't stay here. They need to go. I already hate when you have them over when I'm awake. Do you think I want them here when I'm asleep?"

"Chill, Robin. It's late. I don't feel like driving them all the way back to the club."

"Shit, I have the Uber app." Robin made like she was going to get her phone. "I'll have a motherfucka named Sam outside in five minutes. And then it's obvious that the hoes didn't shower, but they had their stank asses all on the counters like they pay a bill in here!"

Justin groaned. It was obvious that he wasn't going to be able to have his way, although he was looking forward to another round with the women. But it wasn't like either one of them was his girlfriend, and sending them home now would get him out of getting up early in the morning.

"Call the Uber then," he told her and then looked at the girls. "Y'all clothes are upstairs where y'all left them at."

Robin gave the girls a gleeful smile. She always got her way with her brother, and that wasn't going to change until he had a respectable girl on his arm. Coffee left the kitchen first, seeming to not care that they didn't get to stay the night. Sweet Tea, on the other hand, stopped in front of Robin and put her hand on her bare hip.

"I swear it's always bitches like you looking down on women like me," she said with a sneer Robin had to give the girl props.

Robin knew that if she wanted to, she could beat the brakes off of Sweet Tea, but that would be too easy. Plus, women like Sweet Tea never learned their lesson by getting beaten up. No, you had to hit them where it hurt: their hearts.

"Woman?" Robin laughed in Sweet Tea's face and got so close to her that their noses were touching. "A woman doesn't come into a man's house to fuck for money. A woman doesn't put her bare ass on a counter where other people place food. And a woman would never make a living out of shaking ass and selling pussy. I don't care what the media shows you; all you are is a pastime and a nut to these niggas. Ain't nobody gon' be with you for real. Least of all my brother. He did to you what every man has done and will do: fuck you, duck you, and hit you up again when he wants to pluck you. Bye."

It looked like Sweet Tea had just been slapped in the face by a ton of bricks. Her face twisted up into a grimace and her hand twitched like she wanted to lay it on Robin.

"Don't do it, shorty," Justin warned. "That's a problem that you don't even want."

"Fuck both of y'all!" Sweet Tea said and stormed off.

Robin grabbed her phone from the glass coffee table in their African-themed living room and requested an Uber. She then followed her to the bottom of the stairs but allowed her to go up alone, letting her know that the Uber was a few minutes away.

"You have two minutes to get dressed; otherwise, I'ma whoop your ass like I should have when I saw you sitting on my counters. And I wish you would try to take something out of my brother's room, ho," she told her.

Her words were heeded because in exactly one minute and fifty-eight seconds, Sweet Tea and Coffee were coming back down the stairs with long faces and their bags over their shoulders.

"Just think," Robin said from behind them as they walked to the front door. "You still have a few hours to make some dollars at the club if you make it in time."

Coffee made a face at her while Sweet Tea used to her advantage the fact that she was on her way out the door. She flicked Robin off and spat at her feet before she opened the door.

"Bitch, fuck yo—"

Bop! Bop! Bop!

As soon as Sweet Tea opened the door all the way, three bullets opened her chest up. She was dead before she hit the ground. Coffee, completely shocked, tried to find her voice to scream, but a bullet went right through her neck. Robin dropped to the ground right before that same bullet whizzed past her.

"Rob!"

Justin appeared and grabbed Robin's arm, pulling her to her feet right before their house was swarmed by peopled they'd never seen before. He pushed her in front of him, and they ran back toward the kitchen. He didn't have to tell her what to do; she already knew. Strapped underneath every chair at the rectangular kitchen table was a fully loaded pistol. Robin used to think Justin was too paranoid, but right then she was thankful for his paranoia. She tossed two guns to him and kept two for herself as they posted up on either side of the entrance to the kitchen.

"Who are they?" she called to her brother as she heard the quick footsteps getting closer to the kitchen.

"I don't know. They look like some young niggas," Justin told her. He peeked out to see how many of them there were. "Whoever it is, they want us bad. They sent a mini army in here."

"How many?"

"Eight inside. I don't know how many are out."

"I call five," Robin said, checking the clip of her gun.

"I don't know how that's gon' work when I'm calling eight," Justin said, cocking his gun. "Fuck! My vest is upstairs."

"Don't get clipped then," Robin said just as the first man came through the entrance.

With a loud war cry, she chopped him in his esophagus with her left and followed through with a quick jab to his jaw with her right. He was on his way to the ground when she put her gun to his temple and blew his brains out.

Justin took off out of the kitchen toward three of the men shooting wild shots his way. With the aim of a marksman, he quickly put bullets in the chests of the men on the sides and sent them to the ground clutching their hearts. Throwing his gun at the man left standing, Justin got the young goon by surprise, confusing him to catch the gun in midair. Justin used that as his chance to hit him with a three-piece combo, followed with an uppercut so powerful that he heard his neck snap. Justin snatched his gun back and put two bullets in his face just for GP.

Bop! Bop! Bop! Bop!

He felt gusts of wind as two bullets flew past his head and stopped four more goons from coming his way. He turned his head and saw Robin standing there aiming two pistols.

"That was almost my ears," he said with his eyebrows raised.

"Eh," Robin told him, putting her back on his. "They're too big anyway. Get the car keys before more—"

Her eyes grew wide when her eyes fell on something behind her brother. He was so focused on Robin that he didn't even notice somebody come up from behind him.

"I never pegged you for a nigga who paid for pussy."

The deep, menacing voice made the hair on the back of Justin's neck stand up, only because he knew what was next. He turned around just in time to see Amos aim his gun and pull the trigger.

"No!" Robin yelled, putting her guns back up, but someone had snuck up behind her too.

There was a loud gunshot, but not from her weapons. The last thing she saw before she was sucker punched in the back of her head was her brother falling to the ground.

Chapter 5

The sound of glass breaking in the distance entered Robin's dreams. Her senses awakened and the pain in the back of her head shot to the front, causing her to groan. She went to put her hand to her forehead but found that she couldn't. Her head was nodded down, and she forced her eyes to open. Her next breath was a sharp inhale when she realized that she was tied to a computer chair with a rope so thick and tight she wasn't getting out of there.

"Fuck." She winced at the pain shooting through her skull.

She used the little bit of energy that had just come back to her to pick her head up. When she did she saw that Justin was bound to a chair exactly like hers, and although his knee was drenched in blood from being shot there, she could see his chest moving. He'd begun to stir as well. It was only seconds before he came to. He was probably better off knocked out. If she thought her head hurt, she could only imagine the intense agony he would endure.

Focusing on the scenery around her, she felt her chest become a brick of ice. She recognized the room as one that she'd been in literally only twice: once when it was finished, and the second was right then. She inhaled deeply because there was only one way that Amos could have known that the secret place behind the bookshelf in Justin's room existed. It was his man cave, a place that he would go to clear his mind. Inside there was a black two-seater couch, a computer on a mahogany desk, and a shelf full of books. Sitting on top of the bookshelf was Justin's safe, a safe that held his most prized possessions: diamonds.

"Damn, nigga." She heard a voice that she recognized as Amos's speak behind her. "I thought you liked the bitch. You hit her so hard, I was sure she wasn't going to wake up until tomorrow."

She wanted to turn her head to see who he was speaking to, but somehow, she already knew. She didn't want to believe it, but when she heard footsteps coming toward her and she smelled the Burberry Weekend cologne that he loved so much, she knew it was true.

"Malik," she said right when he kneeled in front of her. "But why?"

"Why what?" he asked in a dopey voice. He was wearing all black like they always did when they performed a job. She guessed that night, she and Justin were the job. There was a time when she thought he was one of the finest men in the world, but right then he looked more like scum. She now understood that the reason he could never take it to the next level with her was because he was scheming on her the whole time. She deeply regretted the night that she told him about Justin's secret room, but they'd been so wrapped in conversation it just slipped out. A separate time, when they were lying wrapped in a set of hotel sheets, he asked her what she would do when she got out of the game.

She'd said, "With the three mil in diamonds I know Justin is going to give me, I'm going to move far away. It will be like I don't even exist."

It couldn't have been hard for him to put two and two together on where Justin might have kept his most prized possessions, and he must have told Amos. She wondered how long the two of them had been in cahoots and how Amos had been able to turn Malik against Justin, a man he called his brother. A ball of emotion formed in the back of her throat, and she didn't know whether to scream or to cry.

"Why did you turn on us? We've been working together for so long."

"Truth be told, beautiful," he said, stroking her cheek softly right before cupping her jaw and squeezing tightly, "I didn't plan this out. It just happened. My nigga Amos came along and just started making sense. I got tired of Justin getting the bigger cut of the licks."

"He was the one who caught the bodies. You always acted like you had too much heart. He got the biggest cut because he deserved it."

Malik nodded his head in a mocking fashion. "Ehhh, fuck that. I put in just as much work as anybody on this team. I deserve more than the occasional ten measly bands a job."

"You forgot the first rule of being a bandit," Robin growled, fighting against her binds. "Never turn on your brothers. And if you hurt my brother, I swear to God you will bleed."

"Oh." He let her face go. "You mean like this?"

On the last word, he took a step to where Justin was, across from her in the middle of the room, and kicked his wounded knee. If Justin wasn't awake before, he surely was then. He leaned forward to double over, but his bonds wouldn't even allow his back to leave the chair. He was forced to stomach the pain, and Robin felt tears well up in her eyes. She'd never in her life seen her brother look so defeated, and she couldn't help but think that it was all her fault. Because it was. If she would have just kept her mouth shut, then none of that would have been happening. Malik then proceeded to pummel Justin's body while he was tied up and couldn't do anything but take it.

"No!" Robin screamed. She was fighting so violently against her restraints that the chair she was in shook. "Stop! Stop it! Coward! You fucking coward, stop!"

Her last word came out as a long, dragged-out sob, and Malik stopped, not because she was crying, but because he was panting so hard. His fists were covered in Justin's blood, and so was the ground by them. Justin's eyes were swollen, and his lips were busted. Robin watched her brother's head nod as he fought to not lose his newfound consciousness.

Amos came around her chair and blocked her view. Placing his hands on the arms of her chair, he leaned in and put his face close to hers. The smile on his dark face was a sick one, and the expression on his face read that he'd defeated them.

"He should have never put you on," Robin spoke through clenched teeth. "I always knew something wasn't right about you."

"Where I'm from, baby girl, there's no such thing as a team. It's every man for himself and, well, that mindset has kind of stuck."

"I'm going to kill you." She said every word slowly and clearly to make sure Amos heard her.

He heard her all right, and the words did the opposite of intimidate him. He laughed. "I think you're forgetting about one key part in this equation, beautiful. You're tied up."

Using his big right fist, he reared back and landed a hard jab in her stomach. She tried to lean forward to ease the pain shooting up the front half of her body, but her restraints restricted her from doing so. Her cries filled the air, but that did not stop Amos from continuing to lay into her like she was a random man off the street. Robin felt like her chest would explode if she got hit in it one more time, and blood had begun to spill from her mouth.

"You should have kept your mouth shut to lover boy about these diamonds," Amos taunted her. "You want to go to a place far away? I have two options for you: heaven or hell."

He slapped her hard across the face with the back of his hand and made her head rock to the right. He reared back to do it again but was interrupted mid-slap.

"Yo. Fuck is going on?"

Arrik stepped through the entrance of the secret room behind the bookshelf with Roley by his side. The way that he was dressed showed that what he saw was not at all what he was expecting. The only thing that was not white on him were his jeans. From the looks of how bloody it was in the room, he doubted that his crisp white button-up and new white Air Force Ones would come out as clean as they were when he arrived. His eyes instantly fell on Justin and the woman tied to the chairs. He was a man who had seen a lot, and he had also done a lot. From what he could tell just by looking at the two bloody people, they must have loved each other very much if Amos wanted them to watch each other be hurt and tortured. Arrik didn't care about all of that at first. What he cared about was the fact that he'd specifically told Amos that he wanted to have a few words with Justin himself; but, from where Arrik stood, it didn't look like Justin could say much.

"Arrik, so nice of you to join the party," Amos said, standing back straight again and wiping the blood from his hands.

"Who is she?"

"Oh, her? She's his sister."

"I didn't lend you my manpower for you to be up here beating on females." Arrik's voice dripped with irritation.

"Don't let her looks fool you." Amos leered down at her. "This one is a deadly weapon. She was there on the job with us that night. She works for her brother."

That alone piqued Arrik's attention. He had no clue Justin had a female working under him. He walked around so that he could get a better look at her, leaving Roley standing by the entrance. Although Amos seemed to have done a number on her face, she was still beautiful. Beyond it, actually. She kind of put him in the mind of Lauren London with her light brown hair.

Her eyes found his, and her lips curled. "You." She scowled weakly. "After we do a job for you, you cross us."

"What is your name so that I can address you properly?" Arrik asked in an even tone.

"Robin."

"Robin Hood?" He looked in amusement toward Roley before turning back to her. "Well, the name is fitting, being that I know you also stole fifty thousand dollars from me."

"We didn't steal shit."

While the two of them were having their exchange, Amos made his way to the medium-sized black Hollon BHS-45E safe. He felt his fingers begin to tingle the way they always did when he got closer to a new challenge. He couldn't wait to crack into that bad boy. In all actuality, he didn't know if he was more excited to crack the safe itself or to get to what he knew was inside.

"I know you did. There is no need to lie about it," Arrik was saying behind him. "The thing is, it isn't about the money; it's the principle with me."

"Principle?" Robin laughed softly as her head nodded. "The principle is that the money was earned. The payment that you gave us did not suffice for the fact that small children had to die. You paid us for one body, not a family. Justin caught all of those bodies, so instead of splitting it with these ungrateful sons of bitches, he should have kept every penny for himself."

"Justin caught the bodies?" Arrik said, seeming to be stuck on that part.

"Justin always catches the bodies," she told him, her chin unwillingly hitting her chest again. "He always puts in the most work. We are his team, and he is our leader."

"Okay." Arrik nodded his head and turned to Malik and Amos. "You niggas care to explain what the fuck she's talking about?"

"You would have never given us the manpower if you knew we ain't really put in no work at that last job," Malik said with his gun already pointed toward him. "And these two motherfuckas are deadly. We wouldn't have even gotten this close to the diamonds without you. Long story short, we used you. We were never going to cut you in on the diamonds."

Boom!

The gunshot was so loud in the room that it seemed to have an echo. Arrik looked down at his body and saw that he didn't have a hole there. However, he looked and saw that Malik's gun was not even pointed in his direction. A choking noise got his attention, and he looked behind him.

"Roley!" he yelled as his friend dropped to the ground, clutching the fatal wound on his neck.

Blood was spewing through his fingers as he jerked on his knees, gasping for air. His lungs filled up with blood, and he stared back, wide-eyed, at Arrik before finally collapsing dead on the floor. Arrik made a move to go to his body, but Malik jerked the gun at him.

"Don't move, nigga," Malik said. "You're going to abide by everything we say until Amos gets this safe open and we split these diamonds two ways. Then you're going to call your dogs off downstairs so we can walk up out of here, and I might be nice enough to kill you quick. Amos, hurry up and get that safe open so I can get my half of them motherfuckas and we can go."

"There's only one thing." Amos's voice was low as he fingered the box. His back was to them all, so nobody saw the sick smile that slowly formed on his face. "The diamonds are only getting split one way. My way."

He was a quick draw, and Malik never saw it coming. He hadn't even fully processed Amos's words when he felt the bullets rip into his body. Amos grabbed the heavy safe and fired wild shots, forcing Arrik to duck for cover so that he could run out of the room. Arrik hopped up and made to follow him, but by the time he had his gun drawn and ready, Amos was gone.

"Fuck!" he yelled when he came back into the room. "Fuck!"

Malik was still writhing around on the ground, holding his wounds. From the looks of it, Amos had hit him in places where he could survive the attack with medical treatment. Arrik saw to it that he would never get it. He stood over Malik, who tried to scoot away, but there was no point.

"You killed my day one," he said, cocking the pistol. "Say hello to him in hell for me."

With that, he unloaded the weapon into Malik's face. A big chunk of Malik's head blew off due to the close range, and by the time Arrik ceased fire, there was barely any head attached to the neck. Arrik breathed heavily and spat down at the body and turned to leave.

"Help us."

He was so clouded by his own anger that he almost forgot about the two other bodies in the room. A part of him wanted to just grab Roley's body and bounce, but looking at Robin, he knew he couldn't just leave her.

"No," she said when Arrik tried to untie her first. "Get my brother. He's hurt bad, and he has lost too much blood. No ambulances. He got hit by a car on his way home from work."

Arrik nodded his head and went to untie Justin first. Eventually, his goons made their way upstairs and looked at the massacre in the room. They all had bags full of things from Justin and Robin's house. When Amos knocked Justin and Robin out, he told them that they could take whatever they wanted on top of what Arrik was paying them for the job. They didn't know it, but that was his way of keeping them out of his way.

"If you motherfuckas weren't so busy downstairs filling your pockets, none of this would have happened," Arrik barked, making a mental note to tighten up. The mistake he made that night cost too much, and he would have to live with it forever. "Get him to the car. Drive him to the hospital. Drive off before they begin to ask questions."

"What about her, boss?" the young goon by the name of Clax asked as he untied her.

"She's going to the hospital too."

"No!"

The voice shocked both Arrik and Robin being that it came from Justin. His arms were around the shoulders of two of Arrik's men, and it seemed as though he was using his last bit of energy to look at and speak to Robin.

"Go with him, Robin," he said. "Please get that safe back. Promise me you will. Before he's in the wind."

Robin, whose arm was around Clax's waist for support, wanted to say, "Fuck those diamonds." But they must have meant something to Justin if he was asking her to go after them. After all of the things Justin had done for her, she just didn't feel right telling him no, even in her weak state. So, she nodded her head.

"Okay, brother."

Chapter 6

"Ouch!" Robin winced in pain when the alcohol touched the small gash under her eye.

"I told you it was going to hurt," Arrik said, grabbing a bandage to put over the gash.

The two of them were at the table in his large kitchen as he played doctor to her wounds. Trying to get her to settle down proved hard at first since she was restlessly waiting for someone to call with news on her brother's condition. A big part of her knew that he would be okay, but a small piece, the one that had the biggest effect on her mood, knew that anything could happen. But when Arrik got the call saying that he was stable, her mood calmed and after she showered, she allowed him to approach her with bandages and cotton balls doused in alcohol.

None of what Amos had done to her caused her to need stitches, but she was still pretty banged up and would need a couple nights of rest to be back at full strength. She kept her phone close to her, because she gave the doctor her number to call if anything worsened in Justin's condition. She didn't dare go to the hospital and disobey his orders; plus, she needed to put together a game plan to get the safe back.

Arrik was treating her the same way a person would treat a child when they were sick, except with Robin he was talking a little bit of shit instead of babying her. "For a motherfucka who dropped four niggas, you sure are jumping and crying like a punk right now."

"Because that shit hurts!" Robin glared up at him from her seat. "And it was five, not four. Get it right."

On the way to his home, she explained to him the events that had taken place that night and the night of the job he hired them for. He was intrigued by her combat-ready skills, and he wished he would have known before all that she was telling him. Not only would he have never allowed Amos in his home, but he would have seen about hiring Robin and Justin full time. They wouldn't ever need to do another lick or hit again.

"There," Arrik said once the bandage was on. "All done."

"You must have children," Robin said when she touched the bandage and felt how perfectly smooth it was.

"Why do you think that?" Arrik was amused by her speculation.

"Because only parents can get these damn things on this smooth."

For the first time that night, Arrik smiled. He put away everything he used to clean her up and placed it back into the first aid box. "I have a daughter. She is upstairs sleeping with the nanny."

"What's her name?"

"Naomi," he said fondly. "She just turned three back in November."

Robin heard the love drip from his voice when he spoke about her, and she smiled. "Pretty. She's lucky to have a dad who loves her so much," she said, and then her expression turned serious again. "Look, Arrik, about your friend, I'm sorry."

"It's okay," Arrik told her. "Nah, it ain't okay. But it has to be eventually. The shit ain't really hit me yet, though, but I have to take the bad with the good."

"What good? Everything tonight was all bad."

"We're still alive, right? Both me and Roley knew the ins and outs of this game, and it could have easily been me on the floor tonight instead of him. Fate ruled in my favor."

He and Robin connected eyes for a second, seeming to have a silent conversation. She'd watched him kill Malik for killing his friend, but somehow, she knew that did nothing for his soul. She would never admit to him the way she and Malik were involved. That was an embarrassment she would take to the grave; plus, there was not even a point in bringing it up.

She studied Arrik's face and guessed that they were around the same age. Still, the creases in the corners of his eyes aged him. She couldn't imagine being a kingpin and having to do everything Arrik had to do to maintain the spot, always having someone gunning for him or trying to manipulate him. To be a king, a thick skin was required. Robin could tell that he was hurting more than he would let on, but she didn't press him. She did, however, grab his hand and press it to her lips in gratitude.

"Thank you," she whispered into his fingers, "for saving me and my brother. For that, I owe you my life. If you hadn't come when you did, things would have been worse than they were."

"No." Arrik's baritone voice was barely above a hum. "If it weren't for me, none of us would even be in this shit. I keep fuckin' up. It's like I want to see the good in people, even when I know there isn't any. I ain't wanna run the streets with an iron fist like my father, heartless and cold. But it's looking like I'm going to have to switch my approach. I can't afford to have niggas thinking I'm soft out here. This is the second time in too short a time that a nigga has gotten one over on me."

"That's why you rule in peace, but you make those who cross you bleed. Like Amos. He will pay for all that he has done. You just have to find that balance," Robin told him and placed his hand on the beechwood table. "And you will. I have faith in you."

"Why?"

"Your eyes," Robin said in wonder. "Your eyes don't lie."

"What about yours?"

"My eyes don't lie, but they hold secrets."

"What kinds of secrets?"

Just that quickly, the tables had turned. She didn't know if she should open up to him, but then again, he didn't know her to judge her, so why not?

"About how I really feel about the things around me. Stuff I've never been able to really talk about. This life that I've been living has kind of masked my true thoughts, you know?"

"No, I don't." Arrik encouraged her to continue: "Enlighten me some, ma."

"It's . . . it's stupid." Robin shook her head and looked away.

"Nothing that you feel is stupid. Ever. Talk to me."

Robin closed her eyes, and when she opened them, she noticed that Arrik had scooted his chair closer to her. He smelled like gunpowder and Acqua di Gio cologne, and he rested his hand on her knee. Somehow the scents and his touch comforted her. She sighed and rolled her eyes and tried to ignore the electric shocks racing through her veins.

"Okay, but if you laugh, I'm going to stop."

"Deal."

"Okay. When I was little, before I knew anything about things that went bump in the night, I believed in magic. I believed in the universe because some things we can't explain. Some things are left for the stars to explain. That's why when my parents died, I just put it to the back of my mind."

"How did they die?"

"One of Justin's old hits came back to haunt him. This was way before I was who I am now. I was just a normal high school girl, you know? I mean, I was bad as hell, but I was normal. I thought my mother would get me dressed for my senior prom, do my hair all pretty, and apply my makeup flawlessly. She was so beautiful. I know it would have made her happy, turning me into her twin." She smiled at the thought. "And my dad? He would have taken a thousand pictures of me and given my date a hard time. Him and Justin both."

"Like Will Smith and Martin Lawrence in *Bad Boys II*?"

"Exactly like them! Oh, my God, it would have been great." Robin laughed softly and shrugged. "But life had other plans for me. It hurt. No, it hurts, knowing that I won't ever see them again. After they were murdered, the cleaners burned the house down. Justin and I had been in such a hurry to get out of there we didn't grab any of our family pictures. So, I just hold them really close in my memory. I'm so scared I'll forget their voices, though. I don't want to forget my mom's laugh or even the sound of my dad yelling at me for getting in trouble at school. It's all I have left of them, you know?"

"Have you forgotten yet?"

"No."

"Then you won't."

"Promise?" She didn't know why she needed to hear him promise, but she did. If he promised, she would believe it.

"I promise," he told her, and that time it was he who took her hands in his. He kissed each one of her fingers tenderly.

"I sometimes think that I don't want this life. Then again, I don't know who I would be if I weren't Robin Hood, robbing the hood. The only difference is I give to myself, not others. I give myself everything that was taken from me. I truly feel that my identity now is what the universe gave to me. I am my own fairy tale."

"I couldn't agree with you more. Some days I want to take all the cake I've saved over the years and dip. But then, it's like, I can go anywhere I want to in the world, far away from here, but it ain't gon' change anything. I am who I am, not because of the shit around me; I'm me because of what's inside. It don't matter where I'm at, this hustle in me ain't going nowhere. It's embedded in my DNA, so I just have to accept it.

"Nights like tonight remind me of how savage shit can get. But times like right now with you remind me of how sweet it can be, too. I should be mad at the world, fucking the city up right now. My nigga is gone. But I'm calm, because of you. Tell me something, Robin: if you believe in fairy-tale magic and all that, what if the stars aligned the way they did tonight to bring us together like this?"

"In tragedy?"

"Even a phoenix is birthed through fire," he said, rubbing the tips of her fingers on his lips. "The most beautiful stories begin in tragedy. This might not be the appropriate time to say this, but has anybody ever told you how beautiful you are?"

She inhaled sharply and tried to avoid his eyes. When she'd said that his eyes didn't lie, she was being serious. She was afraid of what she would see when she looked there. But, still, she wanted to know what she would find. She looked at him and bit her lip, shaking her head. "Please don't."

"Don't what?"

"Look at me like that. I don't deserve for anyone to look at me like that."

"Why not?"

"Because it's my fault all of this happened in the first place. If I wouldn't have trusted Malik; if I wouldn't have thought he was different from other niggas . . ."

She'd finally said it. It was out. She could tell by the way his hand got stiff that he knew what she was implying, and she was afraid the look in his eyes would fade. He had every right to hate her. If she had remained solid, then his friend would still be alive and Justin would not be in the hospital.

Arrik watched her closely. She was so beautiful it made no sense to his soul. Her cheekbones were model worthy, and her full lips pouted even when she wasn't upset. Her long eyelashes accented the golden specks in her brown eyes. The once straight hair on her head had gotten wet in the shower, and now it was wavy. He could tell by her posture that she was afraid of what he was going to say or do. It was true that he would be lying if he said he wasn't a little disappointed, but mad at her was something he couldn't be. Just as she was about to drop her head, he caught her chin.

"Chin up, ma. Right or wrong, always keep your head up. I can't blame you for anything when I too got caught up in greed. Those diamonds sounded good to me, so if I am to blame anything, it's the gluttony of man. It has always been our biggest downfall. There is only one thing that I know for certain."

"What's that?" she asked, and he gave her a sly smile.

"If you had made it to prom, you would have been the most beautiful girl on the dance floor."

Robin felt her face grow hot and the butterflies in her stomach go haywire. As unrealistic as it all seemed to her, Robin felt like she'd known him forever. She cleared her throat and took her hands back from him before she did something freaky, like push her fingers in his mouth.

"We need to find Amos before he leaves town with that safe," she said.

No sooner than the words left her mouth did her phone begin vibrating on top of the wooden kitchen table. Her hand flew to it, and she flipped it over, thinking it was the hospital calling her for Justin. When she saw that it wasn't the hospital, but Donte instead, she answered, realizing that he didn't know anything about what had happened that night.

"Donte—"

"I know," Donte said quickly on the other end. "I mean, I don't know, but I know some shit is off. This nigga Amos just called me and said that Malik turned rogue. Said he shot up y'all crib and Justin told him to go to the safe house."

"Donte—"

"And I started thinking, that nigga Justin don't even let me be in the safe house around all that money by myself. I mean, I know a nigga got sticky fingers and all, but I'd like to think I'm the closest one to Justin. If he's letting anyone lie low in the safe house, it's gon' be me! Or you, of course."

"Donte—"

"So, I play it cool and whatnot. I may not be the brightest jewel in the crown, but a criminal knows when a nigga is about to do some criminal shit, you feel me? He said he's twenty minutes away from the house, and I told him the code to get in. I'm too far away so, sis, you know where he's gon' be. Get there. I'm about to go to the hospital to check on my dog. If he did do some snake-ass shit, make him pay. I *told* Justin about trusting them dark-skinned niggas! I don't care if they came back into style."

"Bye, Donte!" Robin hung the phone up and hopped frantically out of her seat. "I need a gun," she told Arrik. "Make that two. Amos is about to be at our safe house. That greedy-ass nigga is going for the cash, too."

Chapter 7

Amos felt like he was on top of the world. Out of all his life of scheming, he'd finally hit the jackpot. He never thought that he would hit big like that, but Justin's team was just too easy to infiltrate. Justin was just too keen on giving chances, and he didn't see the evil that really filled Amos's heart. He grew up with a mother who told him every day that he wouldn't be shit, which was true to a certain extent. He did grow up to be that way, but now he wasn't shit sitting on $3 million. He wanted to thank whoever Justin had stolen the diamonds from in the first place. Because of them, Amos would not have to do a job for a very long time unless it was just for fun.

The only thing Amos needed to do was crack the safe open, which he'd tried and failed to do multiple times already. He didn't know what kind of safe Justin had, but it was a miniature Fort Knox. Still, no matter, he had nothing but time and no doubt in his mind that he would crack it open sooner or later.

He took greed to a whole different level; like right then he should have been on the road headed out of the state, but no. He wanted all of the money that the team had. To the normal eye, the safe house was just a beat-up old house in the hood. One story, one bedroom, fully furnished. It was the perfect house for a grandma. But Amos knew better. He knew that the house *was* the money. He figured that although he wouldn't be able to get all the money, he would get enough to live comfortably without having to cash out on the diamonds for a while.

When he got there, the first thing he did when he entered the house with the code Donte gave him was pull the hose on the gas stove and allow the gas to fill up the home. When he was done, he went back to the living room and prepared to do what he came for.

"Sorry, house," he said when he picked up the sledge-hammer that he'd gotten out of the trunk of his car. "This is going to hurt."

Just as he reared back and prepared to hit one of the walls in the dark house with all of his might, he saw headlights pull up outside. Creeping to the window, he saw that a Mercedes-Benz had slowed to a stop right outside of the house.

"Shit!" he said to himself, seeing Robin and Arrik hop out of the car, both toting guns. "Donte set me up."

Pulling the weapon from his waist, he thought of the gas that he'd released inside of the house. The last thing he wanted to do was have a gun war there, but if they were going to take him out, they were coming with him.

"It's too quiet," Robin said, aiming her gun as she took the first step into the house. "I don't like it."

"Ain't that his car in the front?"

"That yellow Mustang? Yeah. But where is he?"

She walked down the hallway slowly. The one thing she could say about Amos was that he had the same training as her. She couldn't sense his presence because he didn't want her to, and that made him deadly.

"Stay close to me," Robin told Arrik, but he grabbed her hand and put her behind him.

"No, you stay close to me," he said and led the way into the living room. "You smell that? Gas."

Robin smelled it all right, but her mind was on something else.

"The safe!"

She took off in the direction of it and dropped to the carpet. From the looks of it, Amos had not been able to crack it yet, which was a good thing. She tried to lift it up, but it was too heavy for her. She didn't know how Amos was lugging it around, or why he'd even brought it in the house with him anyway. She figured that the only way that she would get the diamonds out of the house was if she cracked the code. From the corner of her eye, she saw something jump out of the shadows behind Arrik.

"Arrik, watch out!"

But Arrik was already prepared for Amos. He blocked Amos's swing with his arm, and after realizing that it hurt far more than a fist, he glanced at his arm and saw a large cut there. Looking up, he was able to lean back just in time as Amos swung the knife at him again. He took two steps back so that he could tuck in his gun and put up his fists. He didn't want to risk firing his gun and causing the whole house to explode. With calculated aim, he ignored the pain in his arm and prepared to lay into Amos the way he used to do cats back in the day on the streets. With two powerful punches, Arrik aimed for the shoulder of the hand holding the knife.

"Aggh!" Amos shouted in pain and dropped the knife.

He tried to follow through with a combo of his own, but Arrik was too quick for him. He easily dodged the hits and stuck Amos in the side of his ribs and followed through with a powerful punch to the chin.

"Get up, bitch," Arrik taunted him. "You should have just stuck to robbing niggas. You aren't ready for this ass whooping!"

Amos got up quickly and used his big body to run and tackle Arrik to the ground. While the two men brawled in the house lit up by the moon, Robin was committed to trying to get the safe to open. She'd already tried every code she could think of— her birthday, Justin's birthday, their parents' birthdays— but nothing seemed to work. She even put in the day that Justin's pit bull died when they were younger, and other combinations that only Justin would think of.

"Come on! Dammit!" she yelled out in frustration. "Justin, what the fuck!"

The gas smell had gotten stronger, and she was beginning to feel lightheaded from inhaling so much of it. She was still feeling weak from the beating Amos had put on her earlier, and if she didn't get the safe open soon, she was going to pass out right there on the floor.

Think, Robin. Think!

She thought long and hard, and finally, something came to her mind. It was a memory of her when she was five years old. She didn't know if it was the gas or the panic that made the memory resurface, but it did, and she remembered it vividly.

"Big brother, I'm scared of the dark!" the tiny voice of Robin said. "Will you stay the night in my room?"

A ten-year-old Justin sat at the foot of her bed, holding in his hand the fifth nighttime story he'd read her that night. They were both in their pajamas, and all he wanted to do was go and play his new video game before his parents made him go to sleep too. Robin wasn't trying to let him go, though; she was holding him hostage. He wanted to be annoyed, but she looked so cute clutching her quilt to her chin and staring at him with wide eyes. He knew that if he didn't do something to soothe her spirits, he would wake up to her and her quilt at the foot of his bed in the middle of the night.

"Nothing is going to get you," he said.

"Yes-huh!" she squealed. "You told me the man under the bed who likes toes will eat my feet if I go to sleep in here!"

He winced, suddenly remembering that he had told her that. He sighed and set the book down on his sister's soft full-sized bed. For that, he figured he owed her some snuggle time.

"Okay," he said, giving in. "I'll lie with you, but only for a minute."

"You just wanna go play that game so bad," Robin said, scooting over so he could climb in beside her. "I don't know why. You always lose!"

He tickled her tummy for talking smack, but more so because she was right. "You better hush before I call the toe monster and have him come by tonight."

"No!" Robin screamed.

"What's going on in there?" their father's voice boomed from down the hallway.

"Nothing," they called back in unison.

"Look, Rob," Justin said, placing his cheek on top of her soft ponytails, "I was just trying to scare you when I told you that there was a man under your bed. Monsters aren't real."

"So why would you lie to me? I'm just a little kid!"

"Because that's what big brothers do. We help you face your fears, and we fight the monsters for you."

"Well, boy, I'm happy that I have the strongest big brother in the whole world then. You need a gun!"

"You better not let Mama hear you talking like that."

Robin's eyes got wide, and they shot to her open bedroom door. When she saw that the coast was clear, she leaned into Justin's ear and whispered, "You need a gun! So that way you won't hurt yourself killing the monsters for me! You can just get them from a distance!"

Justin laughed at how smart his baby sister was. He had never been the kid who felt burdened by having a sibling. She was his best friend. When he looked into her eyes, he saw his own, and he loved her very much.

He truly felt bad for scaring her, and he thought about how she always chose his room to go to when she was scared, not their parents' room. She would probably be terrified as she tiptoed down the hall to get to his room, but the fact that she made the trip let him know that she had courage in her heart. He vowed to never make her feel frightened again. He would only make her feel safe.

"Robin?"

"Huh?"

"You know what I do when I'm scared?"

"You get scared sometimes?" she asked him incredulously.

"Yeah." He giggled. "Everybody gets scared, silly."

"What makes you scared?"

Justin thought on it and remembered the last time he felt fear. The memory made him shudder and hug Robin a little tighter. "That time last summer when you fell into the pool when no grownups were around," he said.

"You weren't scared. You jumped in and saved me!"

"That didn't mean I wasn't scared. I thought you were going to die or something."

"But I didn't, because you saved me like you always will."

"Yeah, but I kept thinking about what if I weren't there? That scared me more than anything."

"So, what do you do when you're afraid, big brother?"

"Promise you won't laugh?"

"I promise! I pinky swear double-doggie promise! Tell me. I'm dying over here!"

"I say, 'Six, four, eight, two.' Over and over, like a spell, and I'm not scared anymore."

"What?" Robin made a face. "I don't get it."

"Those are the days me, you, Mom, and Dad were born. Dad says that he and Mom used magic to make us."

"*That's how we got here?*"

"*Yes. Magic. He said that the universe and stars came together to make us, and as long as we believe in the magic, there is nothing that can hurt us. Especially on those days.*"

"*Magic? So, we have magic powers like Cinderella's fairy godmother?*"

"*N . . .*" *Justin caught himself, remembering that Robin was only five.* "*Yes. We have magic exactly like her. So, nothing can hurt you.*"

Robin lay there and thought about his words. After a few moments, she smiled big, showing off her missing front teeth. She gave her big brother a big kiss on the cheek before pushing his arm with both of her hands.

"*Okay, you can leave,*" *she told him.* "*I'll be just fine! And if the toe monster shows his big, ugly, stupid face, I'll turn him into a pumpkin!*"

Laughing, Justin got out of the bed and leaned down to kiss her on the forehead. "*You do that,*" *he said, tucking her in.* "*But if you need me, you know where I'll be. I love you, Robin. See you in the morning.*"

"*I love you too, Justin!*"

He flicked on her nightlight on the way out of the room and turned off the overhead light. He made to shut the door behind him. He took one last peek at her. She'd turned over on her side and was mumbling something to herself with her eyes closed. Listening closely, he was able to make out the words she was saying, and he smiled.

"*Six, four, eight, two. Six, four, eight, two.*"

"Six, four, eight, two!" Robin said out loud when she came back to reality. "That's it!"

She started to put the combination in, but behind her, she didn't know that Amos had gotten the best of Arrik. While he had Arrik on the ground, he'd jumped to his feet and kicked him hard in the jaw. The blow stunned Arrik just long enough for Amos to grab the knife and make a beeline for where Robin sat. She didn't even see him coming with the weapon until it was too late. He swung the knife one good time and sliced her deeply from just under her nose in a diagonal motion to right under her left eye.

"Ahhh!" she screamed as she felt the sharp cold of the knife.

Arrik struggled to sit up, fighting through the throbbing in his head. He blinked his eyes a few times, and his blurry vision cleared just in time to see Amos cut Robin's face. She fell back, clutching her face, and Amos positioned himself over her and prepared to bring the knife down on her chest. Arrik had no choice; there was no way he would reach them in time.

He pulled out his Glock 19 pistol and aimed for Amos's heart.

"Die," he said before firing the gun once.

The bullet ignited the air around it, and it looked like a ball of fire was making its way toward him. The force of the bullet connecting with its target knocked Amos back and away from Robin. His body instantly went up in flames, and so did the ground around him when he hit it.

The fire in the house started instantly, and they had seconds before it blew up entirely. The fire spread and separated Arrik from Robin to the point where she couldn't even see him anymore. She was hot, burning up actually, and there was no air for her to breathe. Still, she'd made a promise to her brother. The safe was still in her reach, and she inched as close to it as she could.

Six, four, eight . . . two!

On the last number, she heard the click, and the door flew open. With the last of her strength, she lifted her head to look inside the safe. There, in fact, were diamonds inside, but there was something else there, too.

It was something worth more than the $3 million in diamonds, and she now understood why it was so important to Justin to get the safe back. She reached in, grabbed it, and after staring at it for a second, placed it tightly to her heart. She sobbed, and her tears mixed in with the blood pouring from her face. She was at peace, and she was ready for the hot flames and smoke to consume her.

The universe seemed to have other plans for her.

A set of strong arms swooped her up from the ground, and for a second she still felt scorching hotness, but then it was over. Although the pain from the fire was over, the smoke had taken a toll on her lungs, and she couldn't breathe. Before she was consumed by utter and complete darkness, she looked up into the most honest eyes she'd ever seen in her life. She smiled, letting out her last breath.

Epilogue

He never liked the sound of heart monitors, especially after almost losing his daughter when she was first born, but there Arrik sat, listening to one beep away. He didn't know why he was at the hospital besides the fact that his heart had tugged him there every day for the past five days. She still hadn't opened her eyes, but the steady beeping of the monitor let him know that she was at least still alive. She lay there like Sleeping Beauty, but she was better than that. She was Robin Hood.

After the fire, he managed to get her out of there unscathed by the flames. However, he wondered how she would feel once the bandage was removed from her face. The only things that he could see were her closed eyes and her slightly moist full lips. The doctors were able to stitch her up where Amos had cut her, but they told Arrik that she would need facial reconstruction surgery to remove the scar from her face.

Amos had manipulated them all in a greedy haste that ultimately turned out to be his downfall. Arrik's chest tightened thinking about the person he'd lost in it all. He was still a boss, but now he was a lone wolf. The hardest thing he'd ever done in his life was telling Roley's family that he would not be coming home. The amount of money he bestowed upon them was nice, but it would never compensate for the absence of the man of the house. His life would not be the same without Roley, but he knew that somewhere his dog was at peace. He just hoped that when Robin opened her eyes, she would be at peace too.

"Mmmm!"

From visiting her hospital room for hours five days straight, he was familiar with what that groan meant. Her pain medication was wearing off. His heart tugged, because although she was still unconscious, somewhere inside of her, she still felt discomfort. Instead of calling the nurse, he did what he'd seen her do a hundred times. He might have been a street pharmacist, but in another life, he might have made a fine doctor. He applied the correct dosage of medicine to her IV and listened as her moans returned to quiet breaths.

"You should have called a nurse to do that."

Arrik's eyes shifted to the door in time to see Justin Hood coming through the door. Arrik wanted to say that he was shocked, but he knew that men like Justin didn't stay down for too long. His leg was in a full cast, which required for him to be in a wheelchair, and his face was still in bad shape, but his presence still gave the same vibe. The room was silent as the two men stared each other down: two alpha males, both overprotective of the same girl.

"They would have taken too long to come," Arrik finally said. "You would have done the same thing."

Justin didn't have a rebuttal for that, but he still didn't relax his gaze. "Why have you been coming here every day?" he asked.

Arrik was caught by surprise with that question, and it showed on his face. He didn't know how Justin could have known he was there, especially since Arrik didn't even know that he was up and moving around. "If it's a problem, and you knew I was coming, why would you let me?"

"I let you come and see my sister because it's not a problem."

Growing tired of the "who is the real tough guy" act, Arrik slumped back down in the chair beside her bed. His eyes fell upon her chest and watched it go up and down.

"I know it was you who saved her," Justin told him, rolling into the room and out of the doorway. "For that, you deserve to see her."

"I couldn't leave her there," Arrik told him. "My heart wouldn't let me. I had the chance to get out of there, but I had to go back for her. There is something about her. Robin Hood."

"You're telling me like I haven't been around her whole life."

"The diamonds—"

"They're gone, I know." Justin shook his head.

"Yeah, but when I found her curled up, she was holding this to her chest. Something that must have been worth more than diamonds."

He reached into the pocket of his jeans and pulled out a piece of paper. Only it wasn't just a piece of paper. It was a photograph, and when it was handed to him, Justin smiled sadly. He handled the picture as if it *were* a diamond. In his long fingers, he was holding the only photo left of his parents. It was their Christmas photo, the last one they took while he was at home.

He had just turned eighteen, and Robin was thirteen. They stood behind their parents in the living room in front of the tree. Robin's arms were thrown around their father's broad shoulders, while Justin had a hand firmly pressed on his mother's frail one. At that time, his mother rocked a short haircut with a taper in the back. Everyone joked by telling her she looked like the new and improved Halle Berry and they didn't understand how their father had snagged her. Their father just looked like a plump version of Justin. He often teased his dad about being the reason why he would never pick up a beer. Their smiles said it all: they loved each other, and Justin couldn't have been more grateful for his sister than he was at that moment. She had saved their legacy, and that alone was more valuable to him than any diamonds.

"Thanks, bro," Justin said, shaking Arrik's hand; but he turned his head quickly after.

"It's cool," Arrik said, and then he added in all seriousness, "Even thugs cry. I ain't gon' judge you. After all that we've been through, I might shed a couple of tears, my nigga."

They shared a laugh together, and once it died down, Arrik cleared his throat.

"The doctors said she is stable enough to be moved. I hate hospitals, and I can get the finest doctors to see to both of you in my home. When she wakes up, there is something special I want to do for her. With your blessing, of course."

Justin's eyebrow raised in curiosity. "I'm listening."

Robin stirred in her sleep before her eyes flickered open. She remembered waking up one other time before that, but she was too weak to stay awake. The first time she woke up, she was still in the hospital bed, but this time, she was in a bedroom. She didn't panic, although she didn't know where she was. She let her eyes regain their focus, and when they did, she let them stroke every crevice of the room.

It was huge, and she saw an IV pushed to the far corner. She was glad that whoever had removed it did so while she was sleeping. As tough as she was, she hated everything about needles. The ceilings in the room were high, and there was a crystal chandelier hanging from it. The décor in the room was royal, magical even, and the drapes on the window were pulled back just enough so the light from the setting sun could make the bedroom look even more radiant. The canopy bed she was in had sheer white drapes that were open, and it was so big that it had to be bigger than a California king.

The entire vibe around her was right. She even smelled the sweet aroma of food being cooked somewhere, but something was off. Her face felt heavy, and she didn't understand why. Slowly, she brought her hands up as the memories flooded her mind. Flashbacks of the fire came to her, Arrik fighting Amos, and finally the knife.

"My face," she said with tears coming to her eyes. Her hands delicately touched her bandaged face with shaky fingers. "My face."

"Is still beautiful."

The voice came from the far corner, and Robin whipped her head in the direction of it. She would recognize that voice if she heard it underwater, and she prepared to see Justin's face before he rolled up to her bed in a wheelchair.

"Brother, your leg," she said, seeing the cast. "It—"

"Will heal," Justin told her. "Just like the cut on your face."

"How bad is it?"

"They stitched it up nicely, but there will still be a scar."

"Oh." Robin swallowed the lump in the back of her throat and nodded her head.

"I would say that I would get you some reconstructive surgery if you want it," Justin told her with a hint of a smile in his eyes, "but with the safe house going up in flames and the diamonds gone, I'm broke!"

"Broke?" Robin's eyes widened, realizing that what he said was true. "We're broke? Justin, what are we going to do?"

"Don't worry about that. Just know we will be okay."

"How, nigga? You're in a wheelchair! What are you going to do, rob a playground of kids? They're still liable to kick your crippled ass and rob you instead!"

Justin had to hold his stomach from laughing so hard. He had to admit, he missed her, and he was glad that she was finally awake.

"I think I'm out of the armed robbery game for a while," he told her with a mischievous smile. "What do you think about stepping foot into the drug game?"

"The drug game?"

"Yeah. The money will still be dirty, but it will be a constant flow of it. While you were down, I met with two women who do the same shit we do, Rhonnie and Ahli, and get this: they're sisters. We feel as if we can learn a few things from each other, but I said only if you're up to it."

"Of course I'm up to it, stupid. We're broke!"

"Perfect. I guess it's a go with the Last Kings."

"The . . . the Last Kings?" Robin's eyes turned into saucers underneath the bandages. "How did you . . . When did you . . ." She let her voice trail off.

"Who do you think plugs your man's operation here?"

"My man?" Robin asked and then raised her eyebrows. "Where are we?"

"How about you get dressed and come downstairs to find out?"

He didn't wait for her to answer him to roll away from the bed. He pointed to the end of it, where a beautiful golden dress lay. She was confused, and it wasn't until she looked back at Justin that Robin noticed that he was wearing a tuxedo. She gave him a curious glance, but he put his hands in the air and rolled out of the room to give her some privacy.

"I'll be outside the door when you're ready."

She couldn't help but feel like she was getting set up. With some difficulty, she sat up and stepped out of the bed in her nightgown. She had to hold on to the high mattress until her legs stopped tingling. They hadn't been used in so long that she was surprised they still worked.

After a few minutes, she tried to take a step. When that went well, she took another, and then another, until she reached the end of the bed. She could tell just by looking at the dress that it was a perfect fit, and it was. When she put it on, it hugged her in all the right places and hung all the way to the ground. While she was admiring how long the train of the dress was, she saw the shoes that were supposed to go with it, and she smiled. The Fenty slides were the same color gold as the dress, and they were comfortable on her feet.

"Who painted my toes?" she asked out loud, seeing that her feet must have undergone a pedicure. The white polish was bright, and her toes were flawless.

The final steps were doing her hair and finally unwrapping her face. At the vanity, she pulled her long hair up into a neat, tight bun, and she brushed her baby hair into curled waves around her edges. Once she was satisfied with her hairstyle, she took a deep breath and stared at her reflection in the mirror. A part of her was scared to take off the bandage covering her entire face. But it was something that needed to be done. Slowly, she began to unravel the bandage until it was all the way gone. She counted to three in her head before looking up at herself in the mirror.

She stared in silence for a while, getting used to what she now looked like. She still looked like herself, just with a discrepancy. Her fingers traced the thick scar that Amos had created, and she smiled sadly. She felt the tears welling up in her eyes, and she shook her head, refusing them access to her face.

"You are Robin Hood," she said in a weak voice; so she tried again. That time her tone was firm and strong. "You are Robin Hood, and you have magical powers. Nothing can hurt you." She nodded her head and said again in a whisper, "Nothing."

She remembered the words of someone, and when she stood up, she held her head high. When she exited the room, Justin was right outside of it, just like he had said he would be. When he saw her, the smile that was already on his face broadened.

"You look . . ."

"Damaged?"

"Perfect," Justin said. "Absolutely perfect."

He grabbed her by the hand with one of his and used his other to roll them down the long hallway toward the foyer of the house. In the distance, she heard people laughing and music playing. The closer they got to the end of the hallway, the louder the noise got. When they stepped out of the hallway and into the foyer, she was blown away. She knew where they were, but the last time she was there, things looked different.

To the right of the foyer, past the spiral staircase, was the ginormous dining room. Well, it had been the dining room. The tall double doors were open, revealing that all of the furniture had been removed so it could be turned into a dance floor. There was a big crowd of people and even a DJ playing music. Everyone looked like they were having a good time, and Robin let go of Justin's hand and made her way to the entrance.

"What's going on?" she asked, playing with her fingers. "What is this?"

"Didn't I say," a voice boomed at the top of the staircase, "that you would be the most beautiful girl at your prom?"

Arrik stood at the top of the stairs wearing the flyest gold suit Robin had ever seen, with a gold crown on his neat Cherokee braids. He was giving Eddie Murphy in *Coming to America* a run for his most prized dollar.

Dangling in his hand at his side was a thin golden tiara. It almost slipped from his fingers when he first saw her round the corner. He took in her appearance and felt his heart skip a beat. He watched her watch him stroll down the winding staircase until he was directly in front of her.

She opened her mouth to stammer something, but he quieted her by lifting her chin and meeting her lips with his own. They kissed each other with a deep, longing passion, like two broken halves of a heart connecting at last. When their lips unlocked, Arrik rested his forehead on hers and looked down into her eyes.

"You did all of this for me? But why, Arrik? My face . . ." she murmured up at him. "I'm not the same."

"You aren't," Arrik said. "You're even more beautiful to me."

"How?"

"Some things are left for the stars to explain," he said, using her words. "Your face might not look the same, ma, but you are the same to me. Plus, I might have a thing for chicks with war scars."

She giggled through the tears in her eyes and wrapped her arms around his neck, burying her face in it. Behind them, Justin cleared his throat, reminding them that he was still there. Arrik pretended to stand up straighter.

"Damn, you got me feeling like a corny nigga with all these butterflies and shit, prom queen," he said, placing the tiara on her head.

"Aren't they supposed to vote me prom queen?" she said, pointing at the crowd of people.

"Ain't no competition," Arrik said, not taking his eyes off of her. He couldn't believe how good she looked in the dress he had picked out. "Plus, even if there were, my vote is the only one that matters. This is your prom. You are the only one who matters tonight. Now, come on. I have some people I want you to meet. Once you are back fully functioning, they are who you'll be working with."

"The sisters? Ra Ra and Ashley?" She couldn't hide the smug expression on her face.

"Put the claws away," Arrik said, running his fingers gently on her scar. "You have more in common with them than you think. But, no, we will save them for another day. I had somebody else in mind."

Robin looked to her brother and reached out for his hand to walk in with them. But surprisingly, he shook his head no and winked at her.

"You don't need me for this one. This is your fairytale. Plus, you only have two hands, and it looks someone else wants that one. I love you, Robin Hood."

She didn't know what he meant until she turned around and saw the prettiest little girl standing at her feet. She had smooth mocha skin, and she was the spitting image of Arrik. Her hair was even braided the same. Robin didn't have to ask to know that she was Arrik's daughter, Naomi. She was looking curiously up into Robin's face, and her wide, innocent eyes fell on the scar. Robin prepared herself for the little girl to ask her about the scar, but instead, she smiled and batted her long, pretty eyelashes.

"You're pretty. Will you hold my hand? My daddy won't pick me up, and I'm scared of the loud music."

Robin's heart instantly melted at Naomi's cute little voice. She glanced at Arrik to gain his approval first, and when he nodded, she looked back to Naomi.

"Of course I will, baby girl," she said, taking Naomi's soft, tiny hand in hers.

Clutching on to Arrik's arm, she allowed him to lead the way into the prom he had put together for her. She didn't know where this thing with them would go, but as happy as he made her heart feel, she was willing to go as far as he took her.

Once on the dance floor, Naomi let go of Robin's hand and ran into the arms of her nanny, a stout caramel woman. Arrik and Robin were left to slow dance to Case's

"Happily Ever After," holding each other close. The two of them were the center of attention, and Robin was loving every second of it.

"It feels so . . ."

"Perfect?" Arrik tried to finish for her.

"No." She shook her head right before standing on her tiptoes. "Magical."

They didn't know it yet, but soon the love between them would grow so strong and fierce that only death would tear them apart. The kiss they shared at that moment sealed the deal for them to live happily ever after.

The End

Coming Soon:

The Last Kings 3

From the Mind of C. N. Phillips

Prologue

Don't compare me to none of these fuckin' liars
I'm fuckin' flyer, I'm fuckin' realer
Play wit' me, I'll be a fuckin' killer

I drove as casually as I could through the streets of Detroit: my streets. Everybody who recognized my car waved a hand, but I was too focused on the road to wave back. Nipsey Hussle's voice blessed the inside of my vehicle, and I was alone, lost in my own thoughts, trying to get free. The tinted windows to my all-white AMG S65 Coupe were cracked, and I exhaled the last cloud of Granddaddy Purp before throwing the roach out. My heart was beating fast, and when I saw the dozen squad cars racing past in the opposite direction, I held my breath. Instinctively my hand went to the pistol resting in my lap. My fingers wrapped around the butt and the trigger knowing that if they stopped me, I wouldn't be able to explain the bloodstains on my white Alexander McQueen strapless dress. Even in a dress and heels, I was prepared to go out with a fight.

Looking in my rearview mirror, I saw that they were heading in the direction of the massacre that I'd just left. I released the air that was in my chest, but I still did not relax. The weed was failing to calm my racing nerves as I replayed the last thirty minutes in my head.

"Sadie, what are you doing?" I asked myself. "What the fuck are you doing?" I pressed my foot on the gas until my speedometer read almost sixty miles per hour. I needed answers, and I needed them fast.

When I had gotten to Lexington Matthew's house, we were supposed to put forth a notion that would unite not only our two empires, but the empires of every drug operation in the states surrounding Detroit. We both had things in our possession that would change the drug game as we all knew it, like the two missing pieces of the puzzle. However, as with all things, there were some powerful players holding major cards, and they didn't care much for unity. Not even with the Last Kings. They wanted to solely rule the underground drug ring, and what we had in mind wasn't in their plans.

We were ambushed, and if Lexington hadn't been murdered in the process, I would have assumed that I had been set up. Before we could fully explain in detail the levels of changes that were about to be implemented, Lexington got an array of bullets to the chest. His last words were to me, and they were what had me so confused.

I knew I had to get to my house as soon as possible to get the answers I needed. Tyler was out of the country while Adrianna and Devynn were in Miami handling business. I knew I'd be alone.

I sped the rest of the way until I reached the gate of my home. Ray taught me to always keep my land gated. That way if somebody tried to run in on me, they would be slowed down, and I'd get a warning. In that case, I almost went through my own gate. The security there looked at my car approaching and had their guns out, locked and ready to unload. When I got closer, they recognized my vehicle in the night and lowered their weapons.

"Ma'am, we—" one of the men tried to say, but I cut him short.

"Shut up and open the fucking gate, Sisco!"

He saw the bloodstains on my dress and on my hands; then he looked at my face. Without another word, he hit a button, and soon after, I heard the faint hum of the gate parting. I didn't wait for it to fully open to drive through.

The long, curved road led to the house that Ray had built for me. Once I was within reach, I hit the button on my sun visor to open the four-car garage in the back of the house that belonged to Tyler and me. I pulled in and came to a hard stop.

When the garage door shut behind me, I gripped the steering wheel and let out a frustrated sigh. Letting go of the wheel, I opened the door to get out of the car, taking notice of an oil stain on the concrete floor. I mentally made a note to have somebody look under my hood.

The lights in the garage stayed on for ten minutes by themselves whenever somebody returned if you didn't flick them on manually. I wouldn't need that much time. I grabbed the pistol out of my lap and popped my trunk. Stepping out of my vehicle, I stalked slowly to the back of my car with the sound of my heels echoing in the garage. I wasted no time when I got there. I aimed my gun and lifted the trunk all the way up until I saw the body cowering there.

The young girl also had on a dress covered in blood. She was beautiful, too beautiful to be in the trunk of anybody's car. She would either be an important asset to me or be the reason that a target was on my back. Either way, I needed answers.

"This is the part where you talk, or I put one in your head and two in your chest."